Taking the Plunge

Stacie Lewis

snowbooks

Proudly Published by Snowbooks in 2007

2

Snowbooks Ltd.
120 Pentonville Road
London
N1 9JN
Tel: 0207 837 6482
Fax: 0207 837 6348
email: info@snowbooks.com
www.snowbooks.com

British Library Cataloguing in Publication Data
A catalogue record for this book is available from the British Library.

ISBN 1-905005-45-8
ISBN 13 978-1-905005-45-1

Printed and bound by J. H. Haynes & Co. Ltd., Sparkford

To Gareth,

The best thing about the wedding was that I left with you.

I love you,
Stacie

Prologue: Once upon a time…

"Feel my ass!"

Bernadette looked at her stepmom incredulously.

"Come on!" her stepmom said, leaning over in her chair in the middle of a hotel lobby and smacking one cheek, "Feel it!"

A mild panic brewed inside Bernie as she realised her stepmom had a genuine desire for her to touch her buttock. Her stepmom stood and turned her skinny, muscular frame around to present her backside.

"Ah, thanks," Bernie said, "but um…"

"Ah, come on! Feel it – I swear!"

Bernie reached forward with caution. "Very firm," she noted.

"You know what the girl in the Junior's Department at Jacobson's told me?"

Bernie shook her head.

"She said I have the ass of a fourteen-year old."

"Wow, that's great," said Bernadette.

Her stepmom nodded her head in agreement, all the while grabbing her own cheeks. "And have you seen these?" she said whipping around to face Bernie. She leaned forward and slid her shirt over her well-defined shoulders.

"Yes," Bernie nodded, "very defined."

Bernie vowed silently that when she turned 58 years old she would be satisfied with sagging cheeks.

"Now feel my arm!"

A long time ago…in a kitchen far, far away…with an altogether different woman, Bernadette stands in front of the sink about to pour a bottle of rum down the drain. In our story to follow, she is aged 27, but in this American kitchen, she is only nineteen.

"Can I at least keep the bottle?" she asks, stupidly. The bottle is inlaid with gold paint and drunken, wavy lines of glass. It has a shimmering gold-label that says, "100 year-old recipe". What a shame, she thinks.

Her mother rolls her eyes. "Bernadette – the bottle or the police."

Bernie relents and tips the bottle into the sink.

"A gift of death," her mother says behind her, impressing on her the shamefulness of the situation. "You were going to give your best friend the gift of death for Christmas."

"She likes rum," Bernie said.

"Then she will die."

There was a very matter-of-fact tone to that statement; one that kept Bernie quiet while she finished draining death from the (beautiful) bottle and carried it out to the garbage bin. Her mother kept watch.

"Mom? How did you find it?"

"How?" Her mom sounded confused. She looked at Bernie as if she had simply left the bottle out on her dresser with a big note attached to it saying, "Underage drinker about to consume this," as opposed to wrapped in shirts, inside a box, stuffed in her luggage, packed to go back to college the next day.

"Well Bernadette, I just sensed evil in your closet, and sure enough, it was there."

*   *   *

This is what Bernie and her fiancé Sam are up against. Two women. Both alike in dignity (or lack thereof). In fair Detroit, where we lay our scene.

But this is no Romeo and Juliet tale. No, it is far worse. This young couple doesn't have the guts to end it all. They don't even have the chutzpah to elope.

Oblivious to impending doom, Sam and Bernie are much like any young couple in love about to embark on the adventure of a lifetime. Before long – day three of the engagement to be exact – reality will come crashing down.

If only Bernie had known that weddings are like the blackholes of the emotional universe. Until the planning started, years of resentment and insecurities disappeared into this blackhole, only to resurface when she was thrust inside and unable to escape. There are worse things than planning a wedding, but over the coming months Bernie felt she earned the right to use the phrases "poverty-stricken" and "war-torn".

Of course there is something to be said for aspiring to a dream wedding. A wonderful man – her best friend. An elaborate and romantic proposal. A tearful ceremony surrounded by family and friends who adore her (and him!). A fabulous party with all the trimmings. This is what weddings are all about – right?

If only it were so.

Weddings are all about the Fs: Feuds, Family, and Frustration. Then multiply these by fickle and finicky.

The worst by far is Family. Bernie was contending with her family's two matriarchs in particular. Extreme women in every sense, sometimes manic, sometimes loving, sometimes enemies. Two women, who, though sharing similar tastes (in clothes, flowers, art), pretended they despised everything the other stood for. Worst of all, they pretended they weren't pretending and told whoever would listen that they liked the other. Each woman claimed she was the unfortunate victim of the other's wrath. A difficult situation to negotiate. Combine these attributes with Bernie's upcoming wedding and disaster awaits.

And yet for all their insane qualities, for all the times her friends suggested she not return their calls, for all they were about to do to her, she still loved her mother and stepmother. And she knew they loved her. And so it goes.

A sad state of affairs under which to start. But the real story has more drama even than one would think from such an opening. Before this story is out, Bernie will be questioning the state of her family, her future and her sanity. And she will be drunk. Very drunk.

Wedding Truth No. 1:

That fantasy wedding you've always dreamed of? The one in those magazines? The one you've wanted since you were six? Get over it, sister. It doesn't exist.

I am that woman. I am Bernie. I am drinking. Right now I am sitting in front of my computer, working up the nerve to tell my story, a half-empty bottle of beer at my side. It is five years later now. My wedding has long passed. My fifth anniversary is just around the corner.

I am happy. Marriage was the right thing for me. And yet, the planning was something I have never been able to shake. So much so that I am cowardly hiding behind a narrated version of myself. I've given myself an awful name as punishment, but it is me and every terrible moment is mine.

You may wonder why I would risk telling such a story that paints my relationship with my family in such a light. You may feel my actions reprehensible, but I know something you don't. I know how it all turns out.

It's about time I laughed it all off. And besides, I'm not alone. There are plenty of people out there planning their wedding and wondering where they went wrong. There is much missing from the process that popular culture would have us believe should be there, a supportive family being only one element.

Of course, my situation was extreme to say the least. But even that is beneficial here because this book is not for me; I dedicate it to the engaged. After all, there is no better way to feel less miserable than delighting in the misery of others. Why else would soap operas be so popular?

Chapter One: Loaded for Love

They were young. They were single. They were drunk.

In fairytale romances, people fall in love during magical moments. Words like *destiny* and *first sight* get batted around.

In reality, Sam and Bernie were wasted.

When she had arrived at the University of London months earlier, Bernie prepared herself for long hours of study, piles of books and no social life. During her undergraduate degree in Michigan, she was required to read a book a week for every class, and lessons were held every day. Here, on her MA course, lessons were held Tuesday through Thursday from 5-7pm. Independent study was encouraged, along with close analysis of a smaller canon of texts.

Even after spending the whole of her days studying under the vaulted ceilings of the university's library, this still left Bernie with a great deal of time to enjoy her nights out at the student union and mornings sleeping in. Luckily for her, these were all activities her new best friend and fellow MA student, Sam, enjoyed too.

On this particular day, after months of work, both Sam and Bernie received their final grades for the first part of their university course. Both had passed and that meant only one thing.

They were destined to drink, at first sight of the nearest bar.

Later that night, Sam wooed Bernie with a romantic move that knocked her off her feet and on to the kitchen floor – literally. Sure, he liked her, but charging her from across the room and throwing her, and the chair she sat on, to the ground, was not the most subtle of moves. It was the beginning of a clumsy courtship.

Bernie got the hint. The next morning though, in between exchanging awkward looks and rubbing the bump on the back of her skull, Bernie was certain of one thing. Love was the furthest from her mind. "Sam," she said, "I think we should just be friends."

Sam paused for a moment. "Okay."

"Okay? Are you sure? I mean, I just think we are such good friends that this isn't a good idea." She waited for the anguish to gather on his face.

"Okay," he stated matter of factly, then paused again. She thought that his nonchalant demeanour would surely crumble. "So do you want to grab something to eat?"

"Eat?" she asked incredulously.

"Yeah, I'm starving. I haven't eaten anything since lunch yesterday."

These kinds of statements worried Bernie. Could it be that her casual shrugging off a future together didn't faze Sam?

"I'm thinking a cheeseburger, how about you?" Sam tempted.

Bernie declined the offer. She set off at a pace for the nearest phone box to call her best friend in the States. Anne was blunt and flashy, but she had a soft spot for Bernie and her love traumas.

"He just wants to be friends," Bernie told her.

"Well, I hate to state the obvious, but that *is* what you requested," Anne replied.

"But you would think he'd be a little heartbroken." In the background Bernie heard the sound of water. "Were you just on the toilet?"

"Um, yeah. You called me just as I was sitting down."

"You picked up the phone as you were about to pee?"

"Well I saw it was you on Caller ID."

"You took the phone into the bathroom?!"

"Bernie, we've been best friends since we were thirteen. It is not the first time you've witnessed the flow."

"Good point," Bernie agreed.

"Besides, you're changing the subject." In the background,

a toilet flushed. "I suspect you don't want to be just friends with Sam."

"Shut up."

"I think if you keep fooling around with him, you aren't worried you will lose him as a friend. You are worried you will fall in love with him."

"You are demented," Bernie denied.

Anne got louder and more insistent. "AND after you fall in love with him you will want to marry him."

"We are friends, Anne. Friends."

"Friends make the best lovers."

"You are a woman of many clichés, Anne. Goodbye."

"Goodbye Mrs Sam... what's his last name?"

"Goodbye!" Bernie slammed the receiver down.

Now Bernie seriously panicked. What if Anne was right? She began obsessing over the situation. The more she obsessed, the more she told Sam they were just friends. Coincidentally, these conversations continued to occur as she left his bedroom after a night of canoodling.

Bernie really tried to fight it. She went on dates with other guys and told him. His response: "It's your life. We can still be friends if that's what you want."

She tried antagonising him. He ignored her.

She stole his food. He bought enough for her and him.

She dyed her hair blonde. It turned orange. He told her she made a beautiful fruit.

She called Anne. "He's just so nice! He'd give me anything if I just asked. I can't take it!"

"Bernie, you are truly bizarre. Don't you see? He's that nice to everyone. If I wanted dinner, I'm sure he would offer me some too."

Bernie grudgingly agreed. Yet she still persisted in her contrary behaviour.

After all, she was an independent woman. She didn't need a nice guy to take care of her – the bastard!

She did, however, come to the realisation that Sam was drop

dead gorgeous. Sometimes when he turned to her with a big, cheesy grin, sizing her up with his clear, blue eyes, she swore he was a movie star.

But not even this fact of life stopped her from challenging his every move. She was certain even Sam couldn't be so accommodating.

Finally, she hit her brick wall: exam week. Kept enclosed within the computer lab at her London university for hours, Bernie grew more frustrated by the minute. Her final literature essay of the term was due the next day and she saw no end in sight.

Against her protesting, Sam insisted on helping her. She slaved away all day and he spent an hour pretending to look through some literary journals on the pretext of finding an article that would help her. In reality, he spent most of the afternoon swooning in her general direction.

She tried to concentrate under this scrutiny but found it difficult. She was just about to finish a section when she caught him grinning at her.

"Sam!"

"Yes, yes. Okay," he said returning to his research. A few minutes later, he did it again, but this time she tried to ignore him and just continue on with her work. Then he giggled in the chair beside her. She was about to turn around and sock him when he spun his chair triumphantly in her direction.

"I found it!" he cried, interrupting her thought process.

She groaned and swung towards him, her enthusiasm at his great discovery, noticeably absent. "What. What did you find?"

"The article. The one that will finish this whole thing off for you."

"And what's that?" she moaned.

"It's called, 'Radical Departures: How the Airplane Transformed Ideas of Travel in Postmodern Literature'."

"What?"

"How the Airplane – "

"No, I heard you the first time." She turned back to her computer and tried to remember where she had left off.

"Bernie. Don't you want to read it?"

"No."

"No? Why?"

She shuffled papers on her desk, already in the process of composing her thoughts for the next section, but she did pause to address him. "Because I'm not writing an essay on airplanes."

"But there are airplanes in the books in your essay."

"There are no airplanes in my essay, Sam."

"None?"

"None. I'm writing about the relationships between the characters and how they develop against the backdrop of a changing society."

Sam persisted. "But this essay says airplanes changed society. 'Transformed Ideas of Travel'. It says it right there."

"I don't need it."

"But Bernie – "

"Sam!" she snapped, "Okay already! The essay is great! I get it!"

"I'm only trying to help you, Bernie," he said.

Her voice dripped with annoyance. "I said it was great. Can't we just leave it already?"

"You know what," he said, slamming the essay down, "You can just ~~fucking~~ get lost."

He stormed off. Turns out, he wasn't just a nice guy. He certainly wasn't a pushover. It only took that tiny realisation and Bernie fell in love.

Admittedly, Bernie was not accustomed to men being quite so kind to her. But she got used to it pretty quickly.

She dropped the battle and won the war. Bernie and Sam were in love. They both felt like winners. Soon after graduation they moved in together. From a damp, cramped room in the East End, Sam started looking for a job and Bernie started looking for a way to explain to her family why it was imperative she stayed in the UK.

She had two possible explanations to fob them off with: 1) Work prospects were better in the UK or 2) The truth.

Which do you think she chose?

Wedding Truth No. 2:

Just because you are not the marrying type, doesn't mean you won't tie the knot.

In retrospect, everything seems clear. Would I have avoided all the future catastrophes of my wedding if I had just been more up front with my family from the start?

The reality was that I wasn't even truthful with myself at this point. Marriage wasn't on the cards. I got caught up in the excitement of living independently in a foreign country. I told myself that it was London I was enthralled by – its bustling markets, quirky architecture, royal parks and vibrant communities – not some boy.

To admit, not only to my parents, but to myself, that love had a hold over me would have somehow felt weak in comparison to the ambitious, strong, emotionally secure women I was proud to associate with.

But love is not so arrogant. Social standards mean nothing to it. The walls I built around me were only a façade, and I was about to see them collapse.

Chapter Two: The Marrying Type

Bernie had a bit of luck acquiring work. A friend in the States sent web site development work her way and she sold the products off to small businesses in London. It paid practically nothing. Actually, quite literally it paid nothing at all, and she had to take under-the-counter bar work to eke out a living. But she was happy and Sam was happy. Wasn't that enough?

It turns out happiness is not the definition of a legal immigration.

After living in sin together for the year following graduation, Sam and Bernie faced their greatest challenge yet. Bernie had flown home to attend the wedding of a good friend. On the way back she accidentally forgot that her student visa had expired about nine months previously. Immigration was not so forgetful.

"So what you are saying to me is that you can take this disk," the British immigration officer lifted up a CD-Rom helpfully, "and show a company here what your company at home is doing."

"Yes," she said. Windowless and large enough to fit only a small wooden table, the interrogation room felt like a prison. Bernie sat opposite the immigration officer; behind her, a single door led to a cramped toilet.

She watched as he wrote her answer down on a thick pad. "Um… we…" she continued and he wrote down "um" and "we." It was a bit like a long distance call that echoed your own words back at you unnaturally. "We, or rather I," she kept stumbling nervously.

"I show them the disk and note their problems with the design and try to fix it for them on the spot or send it back to the office."

"So what you are saying is that you fix things on the disk here in the UK?"

"Yes."

"And on this disk you can do this?"

"Yes."

"Well that just sounds impossible!" He stamped his hand on to the table. Was she a criminal? There was something really Scotland Yard about this interrogation. Three hours had already passed.

"And what kind of money do you make?" he demanded.

"Sorry?"

"How are you paid?"

"In commissions."

"And how much has that been so far?" he said sternly, still writing everything down.

"In total?"

"Yes."

"I get 15%."

"And what has that added up to so far?"

"Um, nothing."

"Nothing?" he asked in disbelief.

Bernie didn't continue. When you make no salary there isn't much to talk about.

"So what you are saying..." he began again.

After two more hours, he released her to her flat shared with Sam and three others to pack up her things to go home. For good.

Home meant returning to Detroit. Land of strip-malls and even bigger malls. Land of suburban outposts and endless highways. A place a travel book once called, "America's first third-world city." But it was also home to her best friends, her parents and sister who would welcome her back with open arms, convinced all that "London nonsense" was finally behind them.

Oh, if it were so.

Within deportation were the perfect elements for romance: a relationship torn apart, brought together again in the throes of all the possibilities that love brings. Such a circumstance would be the fuel this couple needed.

For this doomed couple, deportation would be a party compared to planning a wedding. That's not to say deportation isn't a serious matter. A relationship breaker. Surely her parents secretly hoped as much. But don't be misled. Destroyer of relationships or not, deportation was the best thing that ever happened to Bernie. Without it, she probably would have lingered in that small shared flat in London for years, scraping by on whatever work she could find and never ever thinking about that word – marriage.

Their friends told them to marry right away. With a marriage certificate, Bernie could stay in Britain. Without it she was not allowed to enter for six months and after that, only with a special visa. But for Sam and Bernie a quickie wedding wasn't an option. However much they took living together lightly, they didn't feel the same way towards marriage.

Bernie's parents divorced when she was five years old, and perhaps they never should have married in the first place. The divorce didn't traumatise young Bernadette, who immediately latched on to the fact that her father was moving to a complex with a pool. Furthermore, with two separate homes she felt secure in the knowledge that she would now have two birthdays a year.

But when it came to her own marriage, she wanted something that stood the test of time. Sam's parents shared that kind of bond. They were an odd couple in every way; he a Welsh eccentric, patriotic and passionate, she a Scottish lady, dignified, steady and maternal; he all silver, unruly hair and ruddy cheeks, and she long, slim and elegant. Bernie admired how, despite their extremes, even when bickering, their affection and amusement for one another was obvious. Bernie loved watching the two of them.

Sam's parents treated her like family from the moment she met them. Thoughts of their home in Wales and the spare bedroom she slept in there, with its musty smell of pine and comforting, quilted bed lured Bernie to sleep late at night after she was deported. In her months away, Bernie missed their kind, generous nature.

Bernie wanted this kind of relationship, one where

companionship would see them through hard times. And this deportation, at the very least, was going to be a testing time.

As soon as they heard of the deportation, Sam's mum called Bernie. Facing such a terrifying ordeal, it was so calming to hear his mother's voice over the phone, even with Sam's father shouting in the background. Typically, he couldn't resist interrupting with some thoughts of his own.

"Tell her we will sort this out!" Sam's father cried. "Tell her!"

"Yes, yes," she responded, assuring him. "Bernie, it's not a problem. Honestly. We will drive down ourselves. Just tell us and we will come to the immigration office. We'll provide a reference. And why shouldn't they listen to us? We are British citizens."

There was a distinct harrumph from Sam's father at this.

Sam's mum continued, "Honestly. No problem. Whatever we can do to help."

In the background, Sam's father added, "Tell her we'll call out the Welsh mafia! Tell her the Taffia will come to her rescue!"

Well, the Taffia never came. Bernie left for America without Sam, without knowing when she would see him again, if at all. She had only her red, puffy eyes, swollen, drippy nose and memories of Sam's assurances that it would all be okay. She believed in him. She believed in them. But that didn't stop her clinging to him at the airport and thinking as she held him for the last time how real he felt in her arms, how warm, how solid. She breathed him in, trying desperately to memorise his smell, how her arms felt across his back, how comfortably she fitted against his chest. He didn't pull her off him even when, as she clung to him, they called her plane. He held her there and kissed the top of her head. He murmured to her and rubbed his face against her hair. Finally, it was Bernie who peeled herself off him. She touched him on the chest with one hand, with the other she stroked his face and kissed him goodbye.

Defying the critics, in their months apart, Sam and Bernie's relationship grew closer. Miles parted them, but they had love and, perhaps more importantly, trust.

During this period, Bernie lived with her mother, biding her time. Some, including her mother and stepfather, may have thought her a freeloader, but Bernie sensed a possibility, yet unspoken, that her return to the powder-blue, lace encrusted bedroom of her youth was not a permanent one.

To this effect, Sam phoned her frequently, late at night, and dropped what he thought were subtle hints. "I always thought we'd have Motown playing at our wedding," he said suddenly to her one night on the phone. "What do you think?"

Bernie gasped. This was the third time he had mentioned weddings in the past month. What was he trying to tell her? She mumbled a musical preference and then sat shell-shocked while he twittered on about which Motown song would make the best first-dance.

"Do you think 'Baby I Need Your Loving' or 'Second that Emotion' would be better?" he pressed.

"Um, I'm not sure. 'Second that Emotion'? I don't know!" Bernie responded.

"Oh, you don't like that song. I see."

"No, no, it's not that." A lump filled her throat. She had to ask him. "It's just – are you trying to ask me to marry you, Sam?"

"No! No." he sputtered back at her. "I just, um, I was just curious. No, no. No–no-no-no-no."

"Right. Then, I guess 'Second that Emotion' is a good choice."

There was a long pause. Bernie's eyes flicked back and forth with anxiety. Had she gone too far? Was he just curious? "I've got to go," she said and hung up. She pressed three on her speed-dial. This was an emergency situation. Anne answered the call. Bernie breathlessly explained everything.

"God, calm down, woman. You sound like you are about to have a coronary," Anne said.

"I feel like I'm about to have a coronary. So what do you think? Answer me. Quick."

"I think he wants to marry you." Anne stated matter-of-factly.

"But really, do you think when he said Motown he meant we'd get married and we would play it? Or do you think he doesn't understand why more Motown isn't played at weddings? Or do you think – "

"Christ, Bernie! He wants to marry you!"

"But are you sure?" Bernie asked cautiously. "Maybe he's trying to tell me that he likes Motown."

"I think he means he loves Motown because you love Motown."

"But maybe —"

Anne moaned in frustration. "I give up. God help me, you are insane. Marry the boy and put me out of my misery."

"But —"

"No buts. Do you want to marry him?"

Bernie was tentative. "Well, I'm not sure."

"What?! Yes or no, woman."

Bernie bit through the nail she had been whittling throughout the phone call. She looked at herself in the mirror. She was a single woman. She lived with her mother. She was at a total loss as to what to do with her future. She could barely pay her student loans let alone for a wedding. But there was one thing she was certain of. "Yes, I do."

*   *   *

So, Bernie tried to prepare her mother for the worst. The worst meaning a possible proposal, a concept beyond consideration, let alone support, from her mother. Bernie's mother had a more traditional view of the world than Bernie. She always aimed for poise and composure, her hair and makeup perfect, her values firmly in place. This meant that the possibility of her daughter marrying a man from another country was impossible, and the possibility of her daughter immigrating to another country and leaving her, even more unlikely.

Bernie's mother had remarried five years earlier. The wedding and reception were carefully orchestrated. To say it went off without a hitch was an understatement. It was an exquisitely beautiful affair. Her stepfather had much to do with this as well. He was an organisational and logistical genius, and she a style and etiquette guru. Together, Bernie's stepfather and mother saw themselves as an incredible partnering, the ultimate hosts.

Bernie approached life in completely the opposite manner. She was relaxed in the extreme and quite prepared to open her door and refrigerator to the people around her. She asked guests to help themselves, a "mi casa es su casa" kind of gal. Where her mother and stepfather would plan elaborate buffets for events as simple as a televised football match, Bernie was quite prepared to partake, but not so interested in reciprocating. This made the concept of Bernie as wedding planner all the more strange to people such as her mother and stepfather. However, more and more, without their knowledge, Bernie began to see herself as the marrying type.

In life-altering times like these, as well as in totally insignificant moments, Bernie often called her sister Beth for advice. Though Beth was younger, Bernie saw her as her equal. Beth and Bernie. Little B and Big B, people called them when they were young, often mistaking them for twins. That didn't last long though. Once Bernie hit puberty, she stopped growing completely and Beth shot past her. Beth was all legs, long and lean. Bernie was her squat side-kick. Beth never seemed to notice this. Throughout their childhood and then into their teenage years Beth's oft shouted, "I'll get my sister if you don't knock it off," was Bernie's call to battle. Later, coming to the rescue of your sister meant something different to both of them. It meant listening to your sister babble on and never, ever turning her away.

"What do I do?" Bernie begged Beth on one of these occasions. Her hands wrapped around an exaggerated coffee mug at one of their usual haunts. "I'm miserable. I love him. They'll think I'm crazy."

"No they won't. They want you to fall in love."

"Not with a British guy." Bernie remembered all too clearly her father's one reservation about sending her off to the UK to university. Before she'd ever set foot on British soil, Bernie made a vow to her father, which at the time, she felt total conviction towards.

Bernie relayed the story to Beth of how, years ago, over the decisive brunch that determined whether she would be allowed to study in London, her father made his main concern transparent.

"What if she falls in love with a guy over there?" her father boomed across the table at her stepmother. Bernie remembered he closed the question by stuffing a half a bagel heaped with smoked salmon and cream cheese into his mouth, then grabbed his newspaper and snapped it open for emphasis.

Bernie's stepmother reached across the table and gently patted Bernie's hand, "You're father is worried that you'll go over there and fall in love and get married and leave him forever."

Bernie stomped her hands on the table. "Dad!" she said, "I'm not going to leave you. I'm going away for one year."

"Yeah, right," he puffed. "You're leaving me and I'm paying for it to happen."

"Oh, let her go," her stepmother said. "This is a great opportunity. She should go. I know you love her, but don't be such a baby."

"Dad?" Bernie said hopefully.

He rolled his eyes. "What choice do I have with two women ganged up against me?" He pointed his newspaper viciously at Bernie, "You can go, but just so you know, you owe your stepmother big time for this."

Having now put him in exactly the position he feared, Bernie looked back and felt the weight of that IOU. Her father would be devastated if she left him for London for good. And who knew what her mother would do. When Bernie informed her about moving to London to go to university, her mother didn't speak to her for three months. What would happen if Bernie told her about her decision to emigrate to the UK?

"It's not going to be easy, but what choice do you have?" Beth said. "You think Sam's going to ask you, right?"

"He seems to be hinting at it."

"Well, if this guy is as great as you say, and he will make you happy, who are they to stop you?"

"They can't stop me, but they can disown me."

Beth slapped Bernie's leg. "You idiot. They're not going to disown you."

"Beth, help me. What should I do?"

"Prepare them. Talk to them about Sam. Make them love him like you do."

Easier said than done. But Bernie tried. Whenever possible, she emphasised her love and commitment to Sam, in order to plant the seeds of marriage in her father and mother's minds. To be frank, nothing blossomed.

"Mom," Bernie tried once over dinner at the Jade Chinese Restaurant, "I just miss him so much." Her eyes peeked over a menu to gauge her mother's reaction.

After this exclamation, Bernie hoped the conversation would move forward in this direction:

Mother: "Of course you do, honey. He is a wonderful man."

Bernie: "Yes he is mother, and I think he may ask me to marry him."

Mother: (clapping hands in glee) "Hurrah! Chinese food *and* a new son-in-law. I am truly blessed!"

Instead her mom shrugged her shoulders and barely glanced up. She was more concerned over whether to order Kung Po chicken or Chow Mein. "I'm sure you do, Bernadette, but let us be honest – you are never going to marry this man."

Bernie went a bit cold. "I may," she said with a faltering voice. "You never know."

"Oh, Bernadette. Be realistic. It's time you started dating someone else, someone nearby, don't you think?" Closing her menu with a satisfied snap, her mother turned to more pressing matters. "Now what do you think about sharing the Vegetable Chow Mein?"

Wedding Truth No. 3

There is no ideal family. Ideals are for movies. The real deal is always more complicated.

One of the most terrible things about weddings is the devastating realisation that they aren't like the Hollywood films. Families especially.

My mother and father tried to be as supportive of my European life as they thought necessary. When I was allowed to go to London, really they were just humouring me. My role was to go to Europe and then become nauseatingly ill with homesickness and catch the first red-eye bound for home.

When I did eventually come home years later, booted out on my ass, I'm sure they hoped I would leave that world behind.

I must admit, I didn't even try. I developed totally evasive techniques to disguise my desires. These techniques weren't that sophisticated. Basically I just never brought it up.

And they didn't either. Yet, I always expected that at some point we would all sit down and discuss it and they would understand the deep levels of emotion I felt and support me wholeheartedly and beg to spend more time with him and thrill to the idea of us being together and all that kind of Hollywood malarkey.

Fat chance.

Chapter Three: Bride of the Year

Limbo: (n.) a state of in-between; to hold on without a foreseeable end; to lie in state awaiting rescue. *(i.e. Bernie's life)*

The Limbo: (n.) a dance competition whereby the participants bend over backwards to win a prize. *(i.e. Bernie's life)*

* * *

Strangely, Bernie's fortunes had turned since deportation. At first she thought it was for the better. In fact, she achieved the impossible in her mind; after months of languishing in her mother's home, she'd finally acquired a full-time position in the marketing department of a magazine publisher. Then, months later, after endlessly tedious days spent moving pixels on a screen and pretending not to check her emails, finally someone on the editorial team recognised her potential and moved her over to their side, the good side of the office. She was now an editorial assistant. A writer! Her whole life, Bernie wanted to be a writer. True, they moved her because of her web editing skills, but she didn't care. She was in.

Of course, it didn't work out the way she'd hoped. Glen, her dumpy boss, balding and sweaty, ignored her pleas to write. With backhanded compliments he'd tell her, "But you're so good at that web site. Why would you want to waste your time on some silly article? Why don't you back-up our issues archives database if you are bored?"

No one understood the web site except her, and she knew it took an entire half-hour of her day to upload. That left 6 ½ hours to fill. She begged for work. Nothing. She brought him ideas. Nothing. It seemed they had faith in her as a web editor, but not as an editorial assistant.

If Bernie wasn't in limbo, then she was in purgatory. Was she meant to be condemned to a life in Detroit? Confined to the dullest of jobs in a mirrored, air-conditioned skyscraper, grey shoebox cubicle and dinky atrium to escape to? Or would she be whisked off to her idea of heaven, living in London, married to Sam?

Bernie took no chances. As she wasn't engaged, her life was currently the former: purgatory. Deported and condemned, she spent her days stuck working for the automotive trade magazine in the aforementioned glass monstrosity. Her fantasy of being whisked off to London seemed to float further and further away with each article she uploaded to the website.

Bernie drowned in impatience. If Sam wanted to get engaged, she would start applying for a teaching training placement at a London university for September. True, she loved writing, but the magazine gave her no opportunities to do it.

Bernie asked herself that question many women do at key points in their life. Not: Do I choose him or my dream job? But: What is the point of a perfect job, a perfect life, if I have no one I love to share it with? She decided if Sam asked, she'd rather spend a year training to be a teacher so she could live with him (this time legally, as a student) than live apart.

Why teaching? Bernie's interest in teaching had always been there. She loved kids; she loved literature; she hated the idea of a "real job." Bernie went to such extremes to avoid a full-time job after her Bachelor's degree that she worked part-time in three different professions, receptionist, babysitter and pizza delivery girl, to make ends meet. Everything about her screamed 'teacher', and sometimes that's enough to scare a woman. She was still young, some might even say immature. Bernie wanted freedom of choice, endless possibilities – not a life preordained. But when faced with an opportunity to quit her exceptionally dull work at the magazine and live legally in the UK with Sam, her resolve crumbled.

Bernie imagined breaking the news to her parents gently; giving them months to get used to it. Giving herself time to get used to it.

Unfortunately, wistful thoughts mulled over while bored at work do not equal an actual engagement.

Not that reality ever stopped Bernie from making plans. Instead, her boredom led to extended daydreams, which led to her jotting down a few notes to herself, which became a list of wedding possibilities, which became a journal entry, which led to her being named a finalist in the 'Bride of the Year' competition for a major magazine.

How did this happen? Six and a half hours were a lot to fill in her cubicle each day. Pretending to work on the web site only took so long. Her job was the perfect ruse to write for real: she had all the time in the world, a computer she was meant to be typing on, a chair opposite the printer and coffee room and a boss who barred himself in his office all day. Perfect.

The competition was irresistible. The prize: a year's writing contract, the chance to have her writing viewed by thousands of people. It was exactly what she was looking for. There was the small issue of the engagement, but as far as Bernie was concerned, she was in purgatory and the devil was in the details.

Never one to be put off by small technicalities, Bernie spent an afternoon in the office, composing an entry she hoped both suitably romantic and quirky for the magazine's readership:

When I applied for a Masters degree at the University of London, falling in love was far from my mind. I didn't just fall in love with the country; I also fell for a classmate. Somehow I managed to stay on well past my degree, but then, like all visas, mine had a limit. After two years in the U.K., immigration decided I'd had enough Britannia for any one American and sent me packing.

Sam and I have been apart for a year now, and I think when British Airways and BT have board meetings, they base their profit margins on our patronage.

This September I'll be moving back to London to join my fiancé. Like all brides, I am excited and this time my visa will have no limitations since being engaged is (no lie) an official immigration status.

Over the next year, I will not only be planning my wedding, but moving country and starting a new career, so at the very least my wedding should provide a lot of entertainment to your readers, but hopefully it will also show how it's possible for a dream to come true even against all odds.

My story will have more twists and turns than a country road and more drama than a soap opera. And since I only recently got engaged, I'll be able to share practically every bit of news.

An innocent afternoon daydreaming about her possible future with Sam – what was the harm? She sent it off and promptly forgot about it.

A month later and she was in the finals.

"Congratulations, Bernie," the email from the editor of the magazine began. "Over 2000 brides applied to be 'Bride of the Year' but only six made it into the finals. You are one of those women. We'd like to set up a time for a phone interview before we come to our final decision. Please email us an appropriate time and your phone number. Again, congratulations and in the meantime check out the web site where you are listed along with all the semi finalists."

Bernie controlled her gag reflex and clicked on the hyperlink. Alongside the five other finalists was her mug. "Click here to learn more about Bride #3: Bernie!" Oh, why had she sent in her photo! Why had she sent in the entry at all?

Bernie felt a rising panic. What would Sam think? Nausea swept over her in waves. She didn't think she'd have any worries convincing her boss she was ill. She stumbled into his office.

He looked her up and down with the mild disgust of a hypochondriac. "Geez, Bernadette. You look green! Are you okay?" He waved his hands. "Don't come any closer if you're not."

"Glen, I have to leave work. I think I'm going to be sick." She pivoted and raced from the office and into the elevator, then straight out into her car and off to Anne's. Early ambition meant that Anne, only in her late-twenties, worked from home, freelancing to television production companies for obscene amounts of money. When Bernie squealed her car into Anne's drive, Anne was sunbathing.

Anne cocked her sunglasses low on her nose and then back up. "I'm hard at work," she said. "What's up?"

Breathless Bernie paced around her. "Me... entry... Bride of the Year... finalist."

"What?" Anne was interested. She propped herself up on her elbows.

"I entered a competition to be Bride of the Year."

"Why would you do that?"

"I wanted a writing gig. That's the prize. The winner writes articles for the magazine about planning her wedding."

"Fair enough." Anne lay back down. "So what's the problem?"

"The problem is I'm not engaged, Anne!"

"So?"

"So, I'm a finalist! I'm posted on the site! My face! My name! Not married!"

Anne leapt to her feet. "Wait. You're a finalist?"

"Yes!" Bernie screamed in exasperation.

Anne screamed with excitement. "Oh my God! This is fantastic! You're going to be famous!"

"Anne..."

"Will they pay you?"

"Anne – "

"Will you get to mention your best friend?"

"Anne!"

"I mean me, of course."

Bernie was waving her arms in front of Anne's face. "Hello?" she cried.

Anne pulled her sunglasses off. "What? What's the problem?"

"Anne, I'm not engaged!"

Anne laughed. "Easily rectified. Call Sam. Tell him to hurry up."

Bernie sunk to her knees. "Oh, God."

"Wait, I get it," Anne broke into hysterical laughter. "You haven't told Sam about this, have you?" She bent over in fits of giggles. "Can I be there when you do it?" she said, wiping tears from her eyes. "I have international calling on my line."

"Now?"

Anne bundled her towel, lotion and book under her arm and trudged into the house. She thrust the phone in Bernie's face. "Call."

Bernie took the phone, pivoted and ran into the bathroom, locking the door behind her.

Anne banged on the door. "You know I'll just hang out on the other side of the door listening anyway."

"Leave me alone. Let me have some dignity."

"Sorry honey, you said goodbye to privacy and dignity as soon as you became Bride of the Year."

"I am not Bride of the Year!" Bernie shouted through the door.

"Not yet…" Anne's voice trailed off as she relented and left Bernie alone. She walked back into the kitchen and started brewing some coffee for the inevitable talk afterwards.

Bernie dialled. The phone rang, its sound hollow in her ear. *Much like my daydreams*, she thought.

When Sam picked up, Bernie didn't speak.

"Hello?" he said.

She bit her lip. What would he think of her? This is the kind of admission that would make most men run a mile.

"Hello? Hello?"

Would he break up with her? Would she look back and see this moment as the beginning of the end? The moment when her adoration turned from romantic to manic in his mind?

"Um, hi, Sam," she said finally.

"Oh, Bernie. It's you. I couldn't hear you." His voice sounded light and friendly.

"Sam, I have something to tell you."

She heard his voice change immediately. "Okay, what?" he said guardedly.

"This is going to sound crazy. And I just want you to know I had no intention of it actually happening. I mean, well, there was always a chance it might happen, but there was such a slim chance, and I certainly wouldn't have done it behind your back. Or, I guess, I couldn't do it behind your back since you're involved." She closed her eyes and held her head. She sounded like a lunatic.

"Bernie," he said as calmly as he could, "I have no idea what you are on about."

"Sam, promise me you won't hate me."

"Bernie – "

"And promise me you will think about what I'm going to tell you and not just react."

"Bernie, I won't hate you. Just tell me." He sounded nervous now. She understood why. She decided to be more direct.

"Sam, I entered a competition."

"Oh, God, Bernie. Is that all…" his voice rasped through the phone.

"Um, no. I entered a competition. A writing competition and I've been named a finalist."

"But that's great! Bernie, that's incredible!"

Bernie thought incredible was a good word to describe it. "See the thing is, well, the competition is for 'Bride of the Year'."

A long silence greeted her. She was right. He hated her. "I'm so sorry, Sam. I'm not trying to presume anything. I just wanted to write and I never thought I would win. I don't want to put any pressure on you. I'm not trying to get you to ask me before you are ready. In fact, I don't know what I was thinking. I'm obviously insane."

Sam burst into hysterical laughter. "Well, that's true enough. I definitely think you are a nutcase. A total loon." He couldn't speak. He was laughing too hard.

"So you're not mad?"

"Mad? No, honey. I'm not mad. I love you. You are the sweetest girl I've ever met. Sweet, and a total nutcase." He kept laughing. "So what are the chances you'll win this thing?"

"Slim, I guess. I'm not engaged."

He hooted. "When has that stopped you?"

*   *   *

Was Bernie giving Sam some not so subtle hints that she was ready for marriage? She was surprised to find he didn't seem to mind one bit. Not that she ever doubted he loved her, but on the other hand, they never really discussed marriage beyond hints.

There had always been a kind of unspoken understanding between Sam and Bernie. They seemed to know the other's mind. So while they didn't discuss it, at the same time, they knew the other thought about it. Certainly, Bernie's newly gained celebrity bride status made it an impossibility to keep their intentions hidden much longer.

Alas, Bernie didn't win 'Bride of the Year'. Some low-life photographer from New York did. Bernie read her entries on the magazine's web site with seething jealousy. Over her engagement? Don't be ridiculous! Her envy lay entirely in the lost prize of writing for the magazine. After Sam's reaction to the competition, Bernie was confident Sam would ask her soon.

A month and a half later, Sam got off a plane in that same Detroit airport where Bernie had been greeted by balloons and consolations after her deportation. After a terrible journey and a year since Bernie's deportation, he was fed up. Visiting Bernie a couple of times in the States had been the sum total of flights he had ever taken, transatlantic or otherwise. Being the friendly sort, earlier, during his stopover in New York City, Sam joined fellow passengers as they walked to their connecting Detroit flight. It never occurred to Sam that there would be more than one airline making the journey to Detroit. If he had been travelling the same airline, this would have been a fine move, but he wasn't. Without time to go back and catch the original flight, he bought an overdraft-shattering new ticket. On the plane, he called Bernie from one of those phones that no one ever uses on the back of the seat in front of him, explaining the schedule change.

Sam's new flight arrived a half-hour earlier so Bernie rushed to the airport, arriving at the gate just in time to greet Sam as he raced off the plane. He didn't hug or kiss her. He gripped the top of her arms. "Bernie," he said breathlessly, "I don't want to do this anymore."

Sam spoke sternly and insistently. Bernie sensed what was coming. "Are you drunk?" she asked noting the aromatic tones of lager on his breath.

"No. No-no-no-no." He shook his head, still gripping her arms. He took a moment to breathe. "By the way," he said looking her up and down, "you look gorgeous."

Bernie melted.

It was the kind of romantic proposal that only happens in films. "Bernie, I've had enough of planes and phone calls, letters and emails. I want you in my arms in the morning and at night. I don't want anything to separate us."

His assurances were of their future, defined, together. He talked on about their friendship and love. But instead of memorising anything, all Bernie could think was, "Remember this Bernie! This is important! Stop thinking about remembering it and start concentrating! Bernie!"

It was hopeless. But she was prepared. When he paused for breath, she had his answer.

"Yes," she said, "I will marry you."

Wedding Truth No. 4

Sometimes, the fun of the wedding ends directly following the proposal. Sorry.

Okay, so I was not crowned 'Bride of the Year'. I didn't pass the interview stage. It won't shock anyone to hear my proposal story lacked conviction. If only they'd interviewed me a month later. Then I would have brimmed over with the enthusiasm and details they wanted.

To be honest, it's a good thing I didn't win. My wedding didn't turn into the fairytale that popular women's magazines look for. I did end up writing about my wedding, but it was for a British wedding website. It wasn't that professional an outfit, but I loved it. People wrote in to me about their weddings, an absolute godsend for me. Otherwise, like them, I would have thought I was the only one with problems.

Of course, my wedding did have some fairytale moments. The proposal sure felt like one.

People asked us how we could do it. The months and months apart. The temptations. But it really wasn't that hard. Sentimental it may be, but it is also true: when you trust in your love for someone, and theirs for you, then distance is a small matter.

That trust would be tested just as surely in the months to come. I am lucky. My faith in my relationship hasn't wavered. Over the course of our engagement, more than one person would try to talk me out of it, family and friends. I know I'm not the only bride this happens to. But simply because I had faith in my relationship didn't mean that everyone else would. Those people weren't shy. They let me know it.

As they say in the Olympics (a far more civilised sporting event): Let the games begin!

Chapter Four: Love Bites Back

"Not that you are doing *it*, or anything like *it*, but now that you are serious with this guy – is he your boyfriend? – I just thought that maybe we should (cough) talk about this whole – well, I mean it is possible, I guess that you aren't a virgin – not that I'm interested! But with you moving in together, well I thought I should tell you to use protection."

This was the way Bernie's father talked about sex back when she first moved in with Sam after university. Notice the extreme use of punctuation. And the moral lesson at the end.

This was how everyone spoke of *it* in her family, except her stepmother of course. "You don't want to hear this Bernie," she offered in the midst of one seemingly normal conversation, "but your father and I do get naked."

No, Bernie didn't want to hear that.

As a glimpse into her parents' sex lives, this was farther than she ever wanted to go. And it was the farthest they ever wanted to go with her.

That's why the "love bite" was such an issue.

But before Bernie received that hickey, as they call them in the States, she would have to partake in the act of love. A bystander (thankfully there were none) would have seen two people clinging to each other as they would if hanging off a cliff. Not surprising then that this act of love was shared the night after informing her parents of their engagement.

*   *   *

Bernie and Sam ate little at the small Jewish deli where they met her father and stepmom for brunch. Today was the big announcement. Waves of nausea pre-empted their disclosure.

Bernie pushed around a piece of smoked salmon on her plate and tried not to throw up. Much of her nausea had to do with what she knew she was about to put her family through. Treason was a word that popped to mind. She was abandoning her family to live on the other side of the world, in Europe no less. A place which her grandfather escaped from in the hull of a rusting freighter so he would no longer have to live with seven other children in a one bed flat. Only a daughter who completely hates her family would abandon them to return to abject poverty!

Just to rub it in, her parents were going to have to attend a ceremony in honour of this decision and pay for the celebration afterwards. Was she trying to kill them?

Sam had a different battle ahead. More than anything else, Bernie's father loved his girls. Bernie and Beth meant the world to him. Sam knew that, no matter how much he loved Bernie, he was ripping one part of this close family from the rest. Bernie's father was a larger-than-life character, who could easily intimidate any man in Sam's position. In anticipation, the deli, popular with all her father's friends, was a good venue to avoid triggering the wrath of a future father-in-law.

The engagement hung over them from the moment they arrived. When was the best time to come out with it? Too soon and you were rude, throwing them in unprepared. Too late, with all the pleasantries aside, and you seemed deceptive.

They practised on the ride over but no rehearsal can prepare you for the demolition of a father's heart. As the deli loomed closer, Bernie found herself compelled to answer a typical question like: "So how are you?" as "Sorry Dad, I'm about to vomit." Or normal small talk before eating like: "Anything new with you?" with "Stop harassing me!" coupled with a big strop and storming off to the toilets.

Whilst Sam and Bernie shook with nerves and held each other's clammy hands, her father and stepmother chatted about a recent cruise, seemingly unaware of the young couple's fright.

In a panic, Sam interrupted her father mid-conversation. Bernie's father was making lengthy comparisons between cruise-liners and their food buffets. Sam could wait no longer. "I love your daughter," he interjected. "And I have asked her to marry me."

Bernie's hand jumped out of her lap to clutch his. "And I said yes!"

What is a typical reaction to a daughter telling her father she is about to get married?

Is it: "Oh, God, I think I'm having a heart attack."

Bernie's father's reaction (much in keeping with the "Oh, God" camp) was to clutch at his chest while downing a glass of water.

Her father appeared truly devastated. She'd ruined his life – hey, she'd almost killed him. Her stepmother, however, screamed with glee – which was a very welcome contrast to her father's reaction. It was her stepmother who insisted he hug Bernie, which he did with a grumbled resignation. He wasn't happy. No, not at all. And he planned on telling her again and again and again in endlessly diverse ways for the rest of her life. This was the kind of punishment that years of Jewish guilt had been preparing her for. A sort of natural conclusion.

*   *   *

Bernie's confession to her mother happened in the kitchen of her childhood home. She met her mother alone. Unlike her father, Bernie thought it would be better to give her mother the space to belt her with the true force of a mother's disappointment. Unfortunately, the anticipation of this onslaught proved too much, and Bernie broke down into tears before she got even one word out. Surrounded by wallpapered mauve and yellow flowers, the clean lines of the kitchen seemed ill-prepared for Bernie's total mental breakdown.

It seemed clear to Bernie's mother that marriage wasn't what

Bernie wanted. Her mother wished for her daughter what most mothers do: happiness, security and love. Across from her sat a blubbering wreck. She touched Bernie's face gently, repeating, "But Bernadette, you should be so happy," which, to be fair, is the traditional attitude a bride should have.

But what was this? Where was the emotional outburst from her mother we were all waiting for? Where were the tears, the screams, the hurling of abuse?

Nothing's that simple. Bernie told her mom and her mom reacted as any mother would. She was concerned about the tears, but hopeful it would all work out. To Bernie it was just plain unnerving.

*   *   *

That night Bernie and Sam stayed at her best friend Anne's house. Anne and she had passed milestones together since they were thirteen: first dates, graduation and starting university. Now, for the first time, Bernie moved forward without her.

Anne didn't mind. She lived with her boyfriend, a moody, needy, weed of a man. "Not marriage material," Anne had once described him.

Bernie swung herself out of the car and ran up to Anne. "I'm engaged!" she shouted, finally assured of a positive reaction. Anne reacted, thrilled, "I knew it!" Her boyfriend managed a smile and shared a weak congratulatory hand-shake with Sam.

As a passing note, it is interesting that it's not only parents that can react strangely to such news. Anne's boyfriend caught Bernie on her own later and made a point of telling her, in confidence, that he was disappointed in her for not telling Anne immediately.

"Waiting until after you told your parents was a breach of trust," he sternly stated. "Anne would have told you straight off."

What? People are crazy. Anne rolled her eyes when she heard this. "Look Bernie," she said, "there is trust like you and Sam have, able to withstand time and distance, and then there is trust like my boyfriend and I have."

"And what's that?"

"That's when you pretend to be forthcoming, but one day while your girlfriend is cleaning the spare bedroom, she finds a heap of S&M magazines under the mattress."

"Yuck."

"You got it."

Later that night, after celebrating with Anne and her boyfriend, Bernie and Sam did what any young couple, separated for months and just engaged, would do. They did *it*.

The next morning, Bernie rose from Anne's futon to discover a hickey the size of a 50 pence piece glaring at her from the side of her neck. The horror of the situation only made the men of the household giggle with pleasure. Surely a 27 year-old does not worry about a silly hickey? Anne, however, with years of experience under her belt dealing with Bernie's family, understood the magnitude of the situation and applied much concealing makeup.

"You are so dead," said Beth when Bernie called her sister in a panic. "You better hope that makeup works." Beth may have been younger, but she equalled her sister in parental catastrophes. While Sam and Anne's boyfriend laughed, not understanding in the least what this hickey situation would mean to their mother, Beth did. Beth had plenty of her own stories to compliment this little trauma. She'd dated more punk hair cuts and piercings than even Bernie had.

"I'm looking at it right now," said Bernie staring into Anne's hallway mirror. "The makeup won't work. It doesn't work. There should be a law against calling a product concealer when it doesn't conceal."

Beth laughed. Not with her, at her. "Well, at least I will have the pleasure of seeing Mom's face today at the picnic when she realises you are a sex monster."

Bernie left that day with Sam to meet her family for lunch carrying a picnic, a beach bag and a neon orange circle on her neck that screamed, "Bernie got laid!"

Contrary to Bernie's fears, no one said anything. No one appeared to notice.

Beth was dismayed. "I can't believe it!" she said as they stood watching Sam play frisbee with their stepfather while their mother prepared the picnic. "You get away with murder! If this was me and I had two pounds of foundation plastered on my neck, Mom would string me up."

Bernie felt very good about herself now. "Maybe Mom just sees me as significantly more mature than you. Being engaged can do that you know. You should try it."

"Fat chance, Bernie. The last guy I brought home had blue hair. Mom has no confidence in me anymore."

"What ever happened to him?"

"Him?" Beth said stuffing a potato chip into her mouth. "Oh, he got arrested. And that was the end of that." She wiped her hands, of the chip and him.

"Wow. I didn't know."

"Yeah. Well, I kept it pretty quiet. He didn't do it, of course."

"Do what?" Bernie asked.

"Steal the car. It was his friend who did it. He was just along for the ride."

Bernie shrugged as if this was totally reasonable. "But still, I can see why you guys broke up."

"Oh, that's not why we broke up." Beth grabbed another handful of chips. "Of course I told Mom we'd broken up. The truth is I visited him in a jail for at least a month first. But then he got really clingy and the journey was such a bitch, so I broke it off. He came looking for me when he got out but I hid behind the couch and pretended I wasn't home."

Bernie laughed. "You are a total moron."

"And you, my dear, are a sex beast. You better not tell Mom about my convict boyfriend either or I am so drawing her attention to that mark of S&M on your neck." Beth twisted her finger accusingly at Bernie and walked pointedly towards their mother.

After this exchange, the picnic carried on, and strangely, much like the anti-climatic moments earlier, no one said anything. No one appeared to notice. The picnic continued on without any major catastrophes, aside from a few burnt hamburgers and missed frisbee catches. All this made Bernie feel that perhaps the only one with no faith in a peaceful wedding was herself, not her parents.

Sam and Bernie stayed on for dinner with her family, intending to head off to a film with Anne and her boyfriend afterward. It was a long, leisurely meal during which her mother and stepfather belatedly tried to get to know Sam better. Open and honest, he was receptive to their questions and concerns. The meal embodied calm domesticity. Everything seemed to be going so well.

After dinner, the mood shifted considerably. Bernie's stepfather vanished instantaneously along with the last of the dishes, disappearing to assume his position in front of the television.

In his place stood Bernie's mother, no longer the genial host. She called Bernie and Sam into the living room for a "serious talk". There she delivered the first blow of the wedding. It knocked them senseless. But it was then that they realised "sense" had no place at all in the coming months.

"Sam," her mother began, "when you make love to my daughter – "

Whoa! Stop there!

Make love? These are words no daughter wants to hear, let alone when she is sitting next to her boyfriend, let alone fiancé.

Make love! The woman might as well have said, "fiddle with Bernadette's nipples." If her mother tried to build a greater sense of insecurity, she would have rolled a joint and smoked it in front of them.

"Mother!" Bernie attempted to interrupt.

"Bernadette, let me finish. Sam, when you make love to my daughter, I will not allow you to abuse her," her mother stated with concern and great force.

Bernie was wrong of course. There was such a thing as worse than "making love." A joint might have even come in handy at a time like this.

Please, house, burn down, Bernie prayed. Her mouth made all kinds of unnatural shapes without words or noise of any kind coming out.

Across from her, her mother sat pertly on the edge of the sofa, surrounded by the calming, pastel colours of the room. Her hands were demurely clasped and delicately laid across her legs. Her lips pressed together gently as she looked from one to the other for some response.

But how does one respond to such an accusation? Bernie had no clue. She looked panic-stricken at Sam, but he did not meet her eyes.

Finally he gave the only appropriate response there was. "I love your daughter. I would never hurt her."

Her mom's eyes whipped to his face, a slow burning blush climbing up her neck. "But you did hurt her!"

"Mom!" Bernie finally said. "It's a hickey!"

"It's a contusion."

For those unfamiliar with the medical terminology used by parents to make trivial injuries seem more significant, the following should help. "It is a hickey, Mom, not a bruise!"

"Did you think you could hide this abuse from me with a little make-up?" Bernie's mom snapped.

"No! Well, yes. I guess."

"So you did hide it," she spat. "So you did know."

"But only because I knew how you'd react."

"Well, I reacted the only way I know how to react when someone hurts someone in my family." She then turned her attention back to Sam who remained dumbstruck. "And if you truly do love my daughter than you will make sure this never happens again."

Throughout Sam's silence, Bernie took a small comfort in how he continued to hold her hand. But then, he could have just been paralysed with the sudden realisation of what he was getting himself into.

And finally it struck Bernie, fear and reality. She had considered how comfortable she would feel marrying into his family, but she'd never thought of what it would be like for him to marry into hers.

Wedding Truth No. 5

**You think your parents want you to get married.
They don't.**

A girl expects certain reactions at these monumental moments. In my dream world, my parents burst into spontaneous celebration and started popping champagne.

My stepmother did. She was ecstatic and I remember the relief in thinking, *Well, at least someone is pleased.* My future in-laws were also pleased, but overseas and over the phone. Not the same thing, exactly.

But, even if she anticipates a dismal reaction, no bride expects something ranging from a heart-attack on the one hand to accusations of domestic abuse on the other.

Though my mother would obviously disagree, even claim the two had nothing to do with one another, her reaction to my love bite, and the engagement it represented, was extreme. Few words feel sufficient to describe the weight of this experience (though I would try as a starter: humiliating, emotional torment).

While I continued to make plans afterwards, this was the moment I began to mourn the loss of my fantasy wedding.

At the same time, I never considered the part I played in it all. Why hadn't I just admitted to my mother that I was genuinely nervous about leaving my family for a new country, a new life? I never mentioned how much I would miss them all. I worried that she would latch on to this weakness in my argument and refuse to let me go. What a great plan that was!

I thought I had considered every possible reaction there was to my engagement. God help me. I did not have any idea what I was in for.

Chapter Five: Shoot Out At The Ok I'm Not Speaking to You Corral

Time was closing in. Once she was engaged, Bernie immediately applied for a teacher training programme at the University of London. She wanted to be with Sam and saw no reason to waste any more time. A quick phone call to British Immigration confirmed that regardless of her previous deportation, enough time had elapsed that if she planned on returning she was welcome, as long as it was as a fee-paying student. She would be leaving for the autumn term in five weeks.

Bernie's family's disapproval was harrowing to her. The days before her departure were being eaten up by her father clucking under his breath and shaking his head in disbelief. "Oh, Bernie," he'd say over and over.

Once he veered from this approach to add, "I hope you don't think I'm going to come visit you this year. Once you are married, I'll have no choice, but until then, I can't bring myself to do it."

This devastated Bernie, but she understood. At least her father was honest with her. He still loved her, but he couldn't bring himself to travel to the place that stole her from him. Fair enough.

Her mother, on the other hand, pretended it hadn't happened. Around the house, the mood was suffocating, like they were all wrapped in vast swathes of plastic. Carefully, Bernie and her mother moved around one another, talking little and resisting sudden movements in case of puncture.

The cataclysmic moment happened on one seemingly normal summer afternoon as Bernie scrubbed the upstairs toilet. Her mother arrived home from a weekend shop and stood silent in the doorway, a force of nature. Bernie braced herself.

"And what do you think you are doing?" she said to Bernie.

Bernie thought she was cleaning. She looked around the bathroom to see if something illicit had happened without her knowledge. "Scrubbing the toilet?" she offered.

Her mother fixed her right hand to the doorframe and pointed, shakily, in the direction of the toilet. "No, you are wiping. Not scrubbing. Wiping. A wipe is very, very different to a scrub."

Bernie realised quickly that the toilet was not the issue. "This is how I've been doing it all year. I thought you wanted me to do it this way." Big mistake.

"No! No, no, no!" her mother exclaimed in horror. "You mean you've been cleaning our toilets like this all year?" She thumped her arms down to her side. "Well that is just perfect! You say you value us. You say you value our home, our family. And this is the way you treat us!"

"Mom, it's a toilet. Calm down."

"Everything is just a toilet to you. I'm sick of it. I want you out!" She banged on the frame. "I want you out of our house!" Another bang.

What Bernie wanted to do at this moment was something on par with Scarlett O'Hara's speech in *Gone with the Wind*. She would hold up that toilet brush and cry: "As God as my witness! I will never scrub your toilets again!" Instead, Bernie just dropped the toilet brush into the toilet. "Fine," she said. "That's just fine with me."

It wasn't fine with her. She was lying. But she had too much pride to go back and talk things through with her mother. Instead, she threw a bunch of clothes into a laundry basket and left. She drove directly to the only place she knew people wouldn't judge her.

She arrived on Anne's doorstep, heaped laundry basket obscuring her view. Anne swung the door open for her.

"Sorry, laundromat's closed," Anne giggled.

"Ha. Ha." Bernie said without any sign of humour. "Anne," she said, "I'm in serious trouble." She dropped the basket on to the floor and started to cry.

"Oh, Bernie," Anne said. "What's happened now?"

"She kicked me out of the house," Bernie choked. "She blamed the toilet. I'm a wiper, not a scrubber." She gulped down her tears and wiped her face. "Anne, can I stay here?"

"Oh, Bernie," Anne said, putting a comforting arm around her. "What did you expect? You're abandoning your mother. She was never going to take it lying down." Anne flung her arms out towards the bathroom. "Bernadette, you can wipe our toilets any time. At least someone else would be cleaning up around here." Anne motioned to her boyfriend, lounging in the other room, one hand down his pants while roving cable television stations with the other.

"Anne!" he called out, oblivious to or ignoring Bernie's entrance. "Anne, can you get me a beer?"

Anne rolled her eyes. "See what I mean?"

*   *   *

Being kicked out of the house, with only three weeks to go until London, didn't mean there weren't things to be done. Like time, weddings stop for no man (or bride).

Bernie imagined that after her mother calmed down and came to terms with her engagement and impending move, she would call Bernie. As the days turned into weeks, this seemed all the less likely.

Then, from out of the blue, her stepfather called her.

"Bernie," he said, "I think it's time we meet up."

"Us? With Mom?"

"No, just us."

There was something conspiratorial about it, but Bernie wanted to make up with her mother before she left, so she agreed.

They met on common ground, a restaurant. Bernie loves to eat.

So does her stepfather. Across a banquet table, facing a room full of wedding guests, they would make an excellent tag-team.

The meal went well. The conversation resulted in Bernie and her mom meeting and reconciling. That was what one should take from the conversation. Her mother would refer to this as a "positive outcome". Getting there was another matter.

"Bernadette, I have asked you here today to try to work things out between you and your mother."

"Okay," Bernie said. She was nervous about all of this. He had such a calm demeanour. She could never tell if he was angry with her or not.

"Your mother is very upset about the distance between you." Bernie assumed he meant emotional, even though she had forced Bernie out. "She wants to see you before you leave."

"I want to see her too, but there is the small issue about kicking me out of the house."

"See it from our side, Bernadette," her stepfather said. "You have lived in our home for over a year now. During that time you have never once offered to pay rent."

"Rent? Sorry, I…" Bernie was flustered. She wasn't trying to be cheap by not paying rent, but in typical Bernie-fashion, it never occurred to her to pay rent to live in her own home. She saw his point immediately, but a year on, it was already too late. "Why didn't you ask me? I did chores. I thought I was doing my part."

"You are an adult, Bernadette. We shouldn't have to ask you."

"Are you saying that this whole last year, you have been waiting for me to offer to pay you rent? You never thought to ask me? I would have paid you rent."

"We shouldn't have to ask you." Her stepfather dipped a chunk of bread in some olive oil and stuffed it in his mouth.

"But you've built up a resentment towards me for over a year because I didn't!"

"Yes, and you have to take responsibility for that."

"And you don't think adults talk about such things? How was I to know?"

"You are an adult, Bernadette," her stepfather quickly

snapped.

"I keep hearing you say that, but the fact is, as an adult, when I have a problem with someone, generally I tell them." Bernie defended her position.

The two seemed to have hit an impasse.

"Do you want me to pay you back rent?" Bernie caved.

"No."

"Well what am I supposed to do?"

He shrugged.

Bernie sighed. She felt like a real low-life.

"There is one other thing I'd like to speak with you about though."

"Okay – "

"The thing is your mother and I are concerned."

"Yes – "

"Bernadette. This engagement. What is there to make us think that you and Sam are going to stay together?"

Bernie sighed with relief. This was easy, much easier than listening to someone call her a cheap freeloader. "Because we love each other. Because we've spent over a year apart and stuck it out."

"Well, yes, there is that." He paused, his hands brushing the comment away, as if this aspect of Sam and Bernie's relationship wasn't all that significant. "But the thing is, we don't know much about your relationship with Sam. We haven't seen you together, for obvious reasons, and we are just not sure you realise what a big commitment marriage is. Being married to someone is a lot different from talking to them on the phone every couple of weeks."

"Well, we did live together for over a year before I was deported."

"But…" Her stepfather attempted to control the conversation. But Bernie interrupted, defending her love for Sam to her stepfather.

"And I think we understand commitment. Even though I was deported and we weren't living together, we stuck together and were faithful to our love."

"But have you?" Her stepfather's eyebrows peaked up

triumphantly. Now we were getting to the heart of the matter. It wasn't a question of commitment. It was a question of fidelity. Bernie stared at her stepfather for a moment and then leaned in.

"Do you honestly think Sam has not been faithful to me?"

"No, actually, it's you. Frankly, Bernadette, you've had a lot of men in your life, and how do we know that you will stay faithful to Sam."

Bernie stared at him across the table. Her fingers splayed around her plate as if an earthquake just hit and she needed to stabilise herself. For the first time that evening, she wished she had a beer.

A lot of men? What did he mean by that? Was her stepfather implying she was a slut?

"Sam is not your first and we don't think he will be your last."

Yes, it seemed he was.

Bernie took a deep breath. "I will stay faithful to him the same way I stayed faithful to him this entire year, by not going out with anyone else. I lived in your house. Did you see me bringing men home? How could you get the impression I was dating? Unless you thought I was dating Anne."

"I suppose I can't remember you spending time with anyone in particular," he admitted reluctantly, as if he couldn't bring himself to believe it.

"I could have dated if I wanted to, but I didn't. I didn't want to."

"But how do we know that this time is different?"

"You know because I'm marrying this one. That makes it different." Bernie ran her fingers through her hair. She never thought getting married to Sam was going to be easy, but she didn't see herself one month into her engagement, kicked out of her house and debating her fidelity with her stepfather.

"So, why don't you swing by the house tomorrow," he said matter-of-factly, wiping his hands both literally and symbolically of the whole issue, before gesturing to the waiter for the bill. "Your mother and I would love to see you."

And that was that.

*   *   *

"Do you think I'm a slut?" Bernie asked Anne later that night.

"By slut do you mean the kind of girl who sleeps around with anything that moves?"

"Yes."

Anne seemed to take the answering of this question very seriously. "Then, no."

"What do you mean 'Then no'? Is there any other kind of slut?"

Anne just gave Bernie her usual "come on – are you that thick?" look. Bernie gasped. Anne was right. She was a slut.

Wedding Truth No. 6

Because there are some people in the world who marry for the wrong reasons, your family will believe you are too.

To answer Bernie's question: Yes, there is another kind of slut. There is the kind I turned into. The kind that whores herself out at any cost to have their own perfect wedding day. The kind that compromises her very soul and integrity to wear white and slink down the aisle to the orgasmic sighs of friends and family.

Like many brides, I signed on eagerly for the most undignified of professions. Unconcerned by what my family thought of me, or how it was destroying my relationship with them, I was determined to persevere with my vision.

I was becoming a total wedding slut. It's the oldest game in town.

Chapter Six: Stepmother Steps In

Bernie remained excommunicated from the Church of Mother. Although she was now allowed weekly visitations, her mother still harboured a secret desire to send her lengthy bills detailing her expenses over the past year.

Her mom claimed to feel abandoned and used. Bernie felt miserable but not responsible. She had lived at home with the purpose of spending more time with her family. It gave her an opportunity to share meals and chat while doing the dishes. But Bernie found in her time at her mother's that her mom only wanted to see her when it was a big family moment. Bernie ate meals alone and did the dishes and the thousands of other chores her mother relinquished to her alone.

Bernie understood this. Her mother was devoted to her new family and a new job. This meant that the little time she had was not necessarily Bernie's to share. But Bernie had also thought that the chores were essentially her payment for living there.

Her mother's feelings of abandonment were a different matter. Her mother took this move and marriage personally. That was the real issue. All the rest was nonsense. Her mother found it inconceivable that Bernie would ever leave her. She had spent the past year trying to convince Bernie to strike out on her own and find a boyfriend. And her mother wasn't one to be defeated.

No matter how often Bernie brought up the move or the wedding, her mother showed amazing resilience in changing the topic. She had endless diversions. Bernie had no luck in discussing dates, let alone actual plans. Finally, Bernie decided to forgo the formalities and abandon any hope of her mother helping her with the wedding.

With only weeks to go before she moved to London, Bernie had serious business to sort out. She needed focus. She needed guidance. She needed –

"Oh, I'd love to!"

She needed her stepmother.

"Oh, you poor thing. Your mom hasn't done anything with you? Anything at all? Not even the flowers, caterer or dresses? Not the rabbi, the reception hall or the arrangements for out-of-town guests?"

Bernie wondered if there was anything else.

Her stepmother pushed aside both their lunch plates in an act that showed she meant business. She had just received her life's calling. Out came her planner, address book, and overbearing Jewish mother tendencies.

"Shit, Bernie! We have so much work to do. Have you ever considered the Bloomfield Temple? The rabbi there is my second cousin Brenda's son and he is very good. You'll love him. I'll call her right now to see if he'll do it." Her stepmother reached in her purse for her phone and dialled. "Brenda? Hi! I'm sitting here with Bernadette and we are talking about the wedding! She'd love to have David do the service. Love it!"

While she spoke, her stepmother gestured to the waiter and pointed to her coffee cup. Then she whipped open her wallet and pulled out a small photo of Brenda's family, flattened it to the table with one freshly manicured nail and tapped one head mouthing, "David."

Did Bernie say she wanted cousin David to do the service? Did she say she wanted her stepmother to call his mother? It was like some kind of terrible blind date your parents try to fix you up for in high school.

Her stepmother clicked her mobile phone shut with great satisfaction. "It's settled. He'd love to do it!"

"Did you talk to him?"

"No, but I know his mother very well and they owe me a few favours, so I know he won't turn me down. They better not turn us down. They won't turn us down. Your appointment is tomorrow at eleven." With that her stepmother motioned for the check.

"But don't you think I should discuss this with Sam?" Bernie asked in an attempt to buy time.

"Sam's in London, Bernadette. You are here. You will see him at eleven at the Temple. Oh, and by the way did I mention the Bloomfield Temple does receptions too?"

"Well, we were sort of hoping to have our ceremony and reception someplace historic."

"Someplace old?" Her stepmother frowned.

"Well, old and beautiful. Someplace with history for our guests to see when they come from overseas."

"Oh, well, let me tell you. Your father will not do old."

"No?" Bernie was not too surprised by this, since her father always wore the latest fashion trends, but she thought he would appreciate the nostalgia of a bygone era. His collection of baseball memorabilia was a passion for him and he loved the sounds of Motown. Regardless of her stepmother's claims, Bernie thought her father wouldn't be entirely adverse to someplace "old."

But at the same time, Bernie thought of how her father always stayed at the newest hotels, on the newest cruise liners, drove the latest model of his favourite car. Maybe her stepmother was right. Balancing everyone's preferences in one event was already proving difficult.

Her stepmother persisted. "No. You check out the Bloomfield Temple. You will love it." With that her stepmother signed the receipt and sealed the planning pact. Bernie knew this wasn't going to be a cakewalk.

* * *

Even David, the rabbi, shrugged when he showed Bernie around the Bloomfield Temple the next day. Perhaps he felt a little awkward too due to the pre-arranged circumstances. The temple was a cold and formal place. He pointed to the outside space.

"On rare occasions when the couple want to, we do ceremonies outside." He motioned toward a grassy space off a small, cement patio. It was bogged down in water after last night's rain. "We do have a bit of a flooding problem though so normally we do them inside." She nodded grimly. "But you know you don't have to do it here. I can go wherever you decide on." He looked pleadingly at her. Did the place make him claustrophobic too?

"Well, actually we were thinking of trying to find some place old, er, historic."

"Historic… interesting. Have you ever thought of Greenfield Village? They have all those old buildings like Thomas Edison's house and they have people walking around in historic costumes that talk about their lives. Well, not their real lives of course. They're actors."

"No, I hadn't thought much about Greenfield Village."

"Well you should. You know they have a working blacksmith there?" David added with a little more enthusiasm in his voice.

"Great. That's good to know." Bernie smiled. She had no interest in a working blacksmith, but she did have an interest in anyone who made suggestions as opposed to instructions. David was young, only a few years older than Sam and herself. He was friendly and helpful without being pushy. She realised that this complete stranger could be her strongest ally in the wedding war.

*   *   *

Later that night, Bernie geared herself up to talk with her stepmother. She called Sam for support. It's easy to give support overseas. It's blissfully far away. If something happens, oh well. It's not so easy when you have to call your stepmother up and you know that if she wants something, she is beyond stubborn; she is completely indestructible.

Her stepmother boasted proudly of this aspect of her character. Bernie could see how, in the coming months, this attitude could be an advantageous one. She also saw how this aspect of her character might cause things to go pear-shaped for her. Be careful what you ask for and all that.

Bernie described the temple to Sam. "Okay, the rabbi was really nice, but the place! The outside had the romance of a medical clinic and inside the colour scheme was dark and cream. Dark and cream! I can't even put a name to the colour, some kind of brown-grey barf. For God's sake, Sam! We can't get married there!"

"So we won't," Sam said comfortingly.

Bernie stared in disbelief at the phone. The concept of turning down an offer from her stepmother was frankly absurd. "We won't?"

"No, just tell your stepmother you don't like it," Sam stated with complete ease.

"It's all so simple to you, isn't it?"

"Come on Bernie. Give your family some credit. They're not going to force you to get married somewhere you hate."

"Watch them."

"Bernie!" Sam laughed a little.

"Sam, it's a gift you know. The innocence in your words is so endearing that I shudder at the thought of breaking it. Hold onto it as long as you can." She was jealous that he could sit idly while she dealt with the conflicts at home. Her voice smouldered with irritation.

"Er, okay," Sam said, a bit bewildered.

As she hung up, she realised she and Sam had just had their first wedding spat. This gave her the strength to brave the phone. They were in love. This was supposed to be a happy time. Bernie needed to stand strong and know that Sam stood in her corner. Her stepmother answered on the first ring.

"Bernie! So tell me all about it," her stepmother inquired like an enthusiastic schoolgirl.

"Um, I don't think The Bloomfield Temple is for us," Bernie said straightaway.

"No? Well, let's see when Sam comes in. I'm sure he will love it."

"I'm not so sure," Bernie said in attempt to maintain her strength.

"Well, he's not going to want something old, Bernie. No one likes old."

"They don't?"

"No. What are you going to do, have your guests fall through rotten old floorboards? These places you are talking about are never clean and at any minute they could just go up in flames. I can't believe you'd even think of such a thing when people like your Aunt Angie suffers from brutal allergies. You're not going to stick her in a place with God only knows what kind of bugs and germs, are you?"

Not wanting to discuss how her decision might kill her relatives, Bernie tried to change the subject, "The rabbi was nice though. I liked him. And he said he could do the service wherever we wanted."

"Good. Good. Look, I've got to go, Bernadette. Your father is blaring on the horn outside. He still hasn't figured out the new garage door opener."

"Okay, well I'll just tell Sam – " Bernie was cut off before she was heard.

"I'M COMING! Bernie, I've got to go. He's going to have a conniption. Don't worry. I'll be sure to tell him the wedding's at the Bloomfield Temple. You two can talk tomorrow."

With that her stepmother hung up, and Bernie realised she would need more than a glass of beer to deal with this one.

Wedding Truth No. 7

Parents appreciate that they do not have the same taste as their children, however, they do feel their taste is better.

At this point in the wedding planning, I was frightened. I had no venue, no dress, no mother, and in weeks I was leaving for a new life, in a new country.

Meanwhile, horrible images of windowless halls and grey partition walls that could be "dressed up" with flowers and drapes kept haunting my dreams. I wanted to marry someplace that reflected our future. It would be wrapped in flowers, a garden or gazebo, the blossoms a sign of our hopeful future. From the reception, guests could gaze out at the lush summer foliage and setting sun. A romantic ideal, I know. I was willing to compromise on just about everything, but I couldn't face looking back on my wedding and only remembering a faceless room.

"Why," I asked myself, "Why is this all so important to you? Isn't marriage enough? Do you really need a ceremony surrounded by flowers and a reception in a grand ballroom?"

From the back recesses of my mind, a small voice kept answering. "Yes! And nothing less will do!"

I was so predictable.

Chapter Seven: A Foreign Girl in a Foreign Land

Bernie spent her last few days packing her life away. Even living out of one bag at Anne's, she'd accumulated an incredible number of things over the past year.

"Of course, you will clear everything out of our house before you go, right?" her mother said to her after corralling her into another Chinese meal.

"I'll try."

Her mother reached for the soy sauce adding flatly, "Or we will just throw it all out."

Bernie rolled her eyes and barely managed to mutter, "Okay, I will."

"You have made a choice, Bernie. Now you have to take responsibility for that. Choices have consequences and in this case that means if you are moving, your things go with you."

"But Mom, there's stuff in the house I've had there since I was born."

"Take it with you then if you like it so much."

Bernie played with her food. She found that with a steady hand she could manoeuvre her chow mein noodles into the numbers of her new postcode in London. *I wonder if I could get the letters too*, she thought.

"Bernie!"

She dropped her chopsticks. "Yes, yes, yes."

"Yes, what?" her mother insisted.

"Yes, I'll do it. It's a ton of stuff, but I will pack it away or throw it away. My choice."

"And…"

"And…" Bernie mimicked.

"And it will be clean…"

"Mom don't you want to spend a bit of time with me before I leave? You are telling me this with three days to go. How am I supposed to do it all?"

Her mother brushed this off. She waved her chopsticks in a dismissive circle before continuing. "It's up to you to organise your last days so that you can share quality time with your family. The question is – " She pointed the chopsticks at Bernie, "Is it important enough to you?"

Bernie rushed to defend herself against the strange hypocrisy in her mother's argument. "But with packing and cleaning my bedroom – "

"And the basement."

"The basement!"

"You don't expect us to just be a storage unit for the rest of your life."

Bernie gave up completely. She went back to number shaping. "No, no of course not. I'll do it."

"Good, and there is one other thing. What are you doing about the wedding?"

Bernie dropped her chopsticks for the second time during the meal. "The wedding?"

"Yes. Have you even spared a thought for it? These things don't just happen on their own, Bernie."

"I am aware of that." Bernie struggled to keep her voice steady. "I've been trying to speak with you about it for weeks."

Her mother's voice was confident with its authority. "Well, you must have been talking to someone else because I don't remember you speaking to me."

Bernie knew she could never win this conversation. She made a half-hearted attempt: "Well, I did. Or at least I tried." But was not surprised when her mother responded with a familiar motto.

"Trying is not doing, Bernie."

"No?" Her mother had the great power of amnesia. Bernie tried convincing her again. "Well, I have been doing," she said. "A lot. And in fact I've been looking at venues to hold it with Anne and my stepmother."

"What! With her! Why with her?" Bernie's mother's voice pitched suddenly at a higher decibel.

"I'm assuming you are speaking of my stepmother and not Anne."

Her mother ignored this. "With her! Well that's just great. I suppose she will be running the show now."

Bernie sensed she was teetering on a steep and slippery slope. She lowered her tone. "I just needed to plan it and you wouldn't speak to me about it."

"Bernadette you are incredible! You abandon me and then you let some other woman help you with the event when you know I want to do it."

It did not escape Bernie's attention that her mother kicked her out of the house rather than Bernie abandoning her, but she kept this to herself. Instead she clasped her hands to her head in a life-saving gesture. "Do you want to help me?"

"Yes."

"Then help me," Bernie pleaded. "Make some suggestions. I want your help."

Her mother reached into her purse. "Well, it just so happens that I have my own wedding book here for us to look through. I have lists of all the best people: florists, music, venues…" Her purse was deceptively large, the book was about the size of the table. "…photos, menus, cakes…"

"This is great, Mom, but remember, I only have three days."

"Well I thought that tomorrow we could see this place," she pointed, "and this one and," she flipped the page, "this one and then on Friday we could look at this place and this other one down the road and then on Saturday we could see these two caterers and get the invitations."

"Mom, slow down, I have three days. On Saturday afternoon,

I'm leaving the country. I don't have time."

Her mother slammed the book shut. "You mean you won't make time. You gave that woman time before your own mother, but you won't give me a couple of days."

Bernie sighed in exasperation. "Okay, I'll see places with you tomorrow and part of Friday but not Saturday." She paused and looked up into her mother's eyes. "I'll have to clean on Saturday."

"See," her mother said with a chirp of pleasure, "that wasn't so hard."

Bernie was overwhelmed, to say the least. In one conversation, her mother had managed to make her feel ungrateful in so many ways. It was a talent, really.

*   *   *

Over the next few days, Bernie tried to fit in everything her mother wanted her to do. One by one she loaded her life into boxes and lugged them across town to her father's to put in his basement. There was nothing else to do. She was only allowed two suitcases on the plane. She'd just have to take a bit more over with her every time she flew.

"I guess these will be here until the end of time," her father said grudgingly as he helped shift the boxes from the car into the house.

Her stepmother shook her head and "tut-tutted" while they sweated and heaved near her. "And how long will they be here exactly?" she said.

"A year?" Bernie offered hopefully.

"A year! And what are we supposed to do with our own things in the meantime?"

Bernie looked at the cavernous basement, stacked with every remnant from the 70s and 80s that her stepmother and father had owned and still it was barely used. She thought about the three-bed flat she was going to share with five others in London. Her father's basement was about twice the size. "Again, I am really sorry about this," she offered. "I would take it all but I only have two days to go, and I'm not going to be just down the road to move it."

"A year," her stepmother scowled.

"Oh, leave her be," her father said. "My father left England because he was living in a one-bed flat with 18 siblings. God only knows what kind of place she is going to." He was exaggerating, but it frightened Bernie to think of how close to the truth he was.

Bernie's stepmother rolled her eyes and huffed up the stairs.

"Hey Bernie! Look at this." He lifted up a mirrored portrait of Al Jolson as played by Neil Diamond in 'The Jazz Singer'. "Wow. What a film. You want this for your apartment in London?"

"No, Dad. Not really." He looked downtrodden. "The thing is," she rushed to make him feel better, "my space is really limited for the plane."

"Oh, yeah. Okay. Classy though, huh?" He rummaged through some more boxes. "What about this baseball hat? You think Sam would like a baseball hat?"

"Maybe if it didn't say 'Domino's Pizza Delivers' on it."

He shrugged and put it on. "Thought he might like it." He turned away and riffled through some more stuff. "Remember this, Bernie?" He held a photo of her in her Brownie uniform when she was nine years old. "You were so sweet." He sighed.

Bernie tried to hold back tears. "I'm really going to miss you, Dad."

"Yeah, yeah," he gestured to her, "come here." He put his arm around her shoulders and kissed the top of her head. "I'll miss you too. No more meals at the Pancake House. No more ice-creams from Dairy Queen. No more breakfasts at the deli."

"Is that all I am to you, Dad, an excuse to eat?"

He laughed. "Yep. I'm sure going to lose a lot of weight when you're gone. The London diet." He patted his stomach and squeezed her tight. "You know, if you change your mind…"

"I know, Dad."

Wedding Truth No. 8

To a bride, marriage is a rite of passage into adulthood. To parents, it is a cliff off which their little girl is about to leap.

While my parents' reactions were extreme, I was also a bit delusional at this point. I was still convinced my parents wanted me to get married. No amount of evictions from the home or stubborn huffing and puffing about the planning was going to tell me differently.

To make things more difficult, I had other mental problems. My ideas about marriage were making me arrogant. After avoiding the idea of marriage, and all it represented, for my entire life, now that I was doing it, I expected people to see me with new eyes.

Getting married made me an adult. I could make adult decisions now about important adult issues. I deserved respect in honour of my new found maturity. If my parents couldn't accept my decisions (which, let's remind ourselves, included moving to a different country, with a man they barely knew, to train for an entirely new career while bankrupting myself in university tuition fees and not receiving a salary until a year hence) then they were the crazy ones.

The truth? My parents were paying for the wedding. I had no job and was about to shack up with five other people. My most important decision recently regarded whether to bring my childhood teddy bear with me to London.

Marriage and maturity are not the same thing. I had a lot of growing pains left in this experience.

Chapter Eight: Worlds Apart

"BERNIE!"

"Yes."

"Ber-NIE!"

"Yes?"

"It's your stepmother here. Hullo!"

Bernie lived in the UK for an entire week before the endless phone calls began. First her stepmother, then her mother. One after the other, they phoned daily, each with her own list of ideas, or demands, depending on how you looked at it.

"Bernie, did you know your mother wants to be in charge of the flowers," would be a typical opening gambit from her stepmother.

"She did mention –"

"And did you mention to her that she needed to consult with all of us first?"

"Er, no. I was just grateful for the help," Bernie said.

"What about your father?"

"I don't think my father cares all that much about flowers."

"He does," her stepmother claimed.

"He does?"

"Yes. And he doesn't want cheap, tacky arrangements dotting the hall."

"I doubt my mother does either."

Her stepmother tried another angle. "Do you know we met with the florist? She is the best florist in town. And your mother already saw her before we did. How could you let this happen, Bernie?"

And so it went. One call after the other, one side "getting" to the best florist, or the best cake maker, or the rabbi before the other did. But strangely, each woman wanting exactly the same "best florist in town." So much the same and yet, so different – in China perhaps they would have been seen as the yin and yang of wedding planning.

*   *   *

"Bernadette."

"Yes, Mother."

"You must call your father and tell him I won't be having a sweet table at the wedding."

"Don't you think we should pick out a venue first?"

"You tell me. Your father and his wife seem to think that a sweet table is the biggest concern. They have ordered one and I don't want one."

"You don't? Good thing it's your wedding then."

Her voice curdled. "Bernie, your insolence is not helping."

"Mother, the sweet table is news to me, but to be honest, what's the harm? If he wants to pay for a sweet table, let him."

"The sweet table they have ordered is the size of Ohio," she paused to emphasise the magnitude of the table. "What I mean by that is: it is very large."

"I understood that," said Bernie.

"It is two banquet-size tables long. Everyone will eat candy instead of cake. They want people to eat candy instead of cake. They know I want to buy the cake." She paused and gathered her composure. "But it isn't really about whether we decide to have a sweet table or not, it is the lack of discussion that upsets me."

"Much like going to a florist without them?"

"Now don't you start, Bernadette. You are changing the subject. Why have you not informed me about the sweet table? Why have you let this happen? It is incredibly disrespectful of you."

*   *   *

Bernie wasn't a religious woman, but those first few weeks in London she prayed a lot. "Please God, please: tell my parents to ████ right off." If only God weren't a religious man, he might have listened to such obscenities. As it was, he left her to her own devices.

Bernie reminded herself that she would not be having a wedding at all if it weren't for her parents. Bernie and Sam were living off his salary, which afforded them a room in a three-bed flat and one meal out a month.

A perfect wedding is big business. Romance comes with a hefty price tag. Everything from the officiant to the venue has hidden prices. Bernie found plenty of cheap halls to rent, but serving the guests food was a fortune. Most venues only allow the couple to use their caterers and their wine list, both at Michelin star prices, but not however Michelin-starred quality. The cheapest bottle of wine is always still expensive and they charge you to cork each one. One place even told Bernie they would charge her to put soap in the washrooms.

*   *   *

Bernie had something to be happy about. She was in a different country. She was far away from price lists and squabbling over sweet tables. Unfortunately her mother and stepmother didn't see an ocean as all that great an obstacle.

The phone calls continued in the lead up to Christmas. They gained ferocity rather than diminished. They grew in length and frequency rather than shorten. They were not affected by long distance rates or different time zones.

Meanwhile, Bernie's life continued.

Outside Wedding World, normal things like bills and immigration paperwork still needed to be filled out. Bernie had other concerns as well. She'd just started teacher training at an inner-city high school in London. The program was tough: unpaid, long hours and high expectations. Regardless, it was a relief in some ways to worry about real things instead of hours pondering colours for napkins.

Each day she tried to carve out a niche for herself in the working life of a broken school. It was a tough placement to start in. The windows of her classroom were made of shatterproof glass that only meant they had the appearance of framed spider webs of fragmented glass: broken but not on the floor. The door was spray painted with someone's graffiti tag on the outside, and fitted with the comforting quirk of not shutting, or shutting and not opening once closed. Not an ideal situation when a fight kicks off.

There was a pleasure in teaching that she had not experienced in any other job though. The pressure, the work, the responsibility was an almighty weight, but the all-consuming nature of the job was a gift as well. She felt enveloped in it.

Compared to the whinging she was listening to every night over the phone, the children's real juvenile problems seemed like a gift. Leave it to kids to put it all in perspective.

Bernie made it through her first term unscathed with the help of her student partner Clare. Together they shared resources and pints after work. Bernie updated her with tales about the wedding to lighten their mood.

"You should see the volumes of invitations they sent me to look through," Bernie said after school in the pub one Thursday. "I could insulate a house with them."

"Is there enough for our school? My room is so cold that my nipples froze to my copy of 'Romeo and Juliet' yesterday," Clare said.

"Not only enough to insulate but wallpaper as well."

"Good, because graffiti is SO last year."

Bernie took a sip of her drink. She held it with two hands like she needed all the support it was giving. "Yesterday my stepmother asked me if she could buy me an answering machine."

"Oh, God! You don't want that! Then they'll be able to contact you at all times."

"And I'd feel obligated to call back as well. They already call me every day."

Clare leaned in. "And what did you say?"

"I told her they don't sell them over here."

"Did she believe you?"

Bernie shrugged. "Of course. They think people over here are archaic. How else do they explain the bad teeth and milk in tea?"

"You don't have milk in your tea in the States?"

"Are you kidding? We barely drink tea." Clare seemed genuinely shocked by this. Life without tea, for a Brit, is not worth living. Tea breaks are scheduled into the day, a concept completely alien to Americans. "Of course, I drink at least three cups of tea a day now." Then she added, as if to make Americans seem semi-civilised, "In the States, people drink coffee."

This seemed to settle Clare's concern for the sanity of America. She finished her pint and banged it down on to the table. "Well, Bernie, let me introduce you to a little tradition I'm familiar with. In Britain we drink lager, and the American always buys."

Wedding Truth No. 9

Most families, and even some brides, believe that one's life stops while the planning of a wedding takes place. This is a lie. Life continues.

I was lucky. I didn't believe this lie. It was very obvious, between the move, the new job and the endless parental squabbles, that my life was very much not about choosing lovely flower bouquets and attending cake tastings.

Some brides relish the all-consuming nature of wedding planning. They rise early in the hopes of finding that perfect silver ribbon to adorn the guests' tables or cherish the opportunity to argue over prices with the caterer. Then there are the rest of us.

It is not only brides that can relate to this. For every office worker forced to listen in detail to decisions of paramount importance such as whether there should be a fuchsia spring theme or autumnal red at their colleague's reception. For every groom who spends each meal debating the type of potato (mashed, boiled, parboiled, baked, twice baked, fried, diced, fricasseed) to be served for one meal taking place six months hence. For every friend who is dragged from one bridal dress shop to the next, every Saturday for the next three months.

For each of you reading this: wedding plans are only a brief part of a long life, not life itself.

Thank God.

Chapter Nine: Marriage Mondays

Fights and bickering. Christmas was approaching. Soon Bernie would have to leave teacher training to endure it all again, except this time she would be on holiday and the bullies would be family members.

It was bad enough getting daily phone calls that informed her about the other side's failings. She was not relishing the idea of playing referee in person. Her parents were adults; why couldn't they have an adult conversation with one another?

Her father generously offered to fly her home so she could be there in person to make the decisions. She hadn't wanted to accept, but she could hardly say no. As the piles of sample invites grew, so did the impending decisions and agitation. She vowed to stand firm and not let them boss her around. So why did she feel so weak?

*   *   *

As Bernie's plane left Heathrow airport for Detroit, she felt her stomach drop. Her hand reached reassuringly towards the sick bag. She retracted it and then grabbed for it. Just as quickly her nausea dissipated. It was nerves more than travel sickness.

The air hostess charged her trolley down the aisle a half hour later bashing Bernie's elbow. Bernie instantly forgave her. "Red wine," she said to the woman, "and a whiskey."

She had asked, begged, Sam to join her. It was only four months since that day last summer when her mother had chucked her out of her house and now she was going to have to negotiate flowers and colours with her. Ever the optimist, she cornered him in the bedroom, got on her knees and grabbed hold of his leg. "Pleeeeze," she whined.

Looking down at her with an expression of both pity and amusement he said, "You know I would, Bernie, but we don't have the money. Be realistic."

"Realistic? I can be realistic. What's more important: food or your ticket? Do I need to eat? After all, I'm a bride. All brides diet for their weddings. I need to slim down. Don't I? Please?"

"No."

"No?" She let go of his leg but didn't stand. Instead she plopped down against the bed. Her eyes filled with tears.

"Oh, Bernie," he said and sat down next to her. He wiped a tear from her cheek. "You can do this. We are talking about decisions of monumental importance like whether to have a sweet table or not. I say: okay, fine! If forced, I will eat the damn sweets."

She stopped crying and giggled a bit. "I know I am being ridiculous, but they call me twice a day, every day, how am I going to cope with full-on visitation?"

"I really don't know. Make Anne go for a drink with you."

She patted his knee. "Good advice. I'll drink my way through it."

He smiled and hugged her to him. "Everything is going to be fine," he said.

Now on the plane, she wished she had forced the issue a bit more. A starvation diet seemed so much more appealing than this visit home. Just as the stewardess passed her, she remembered his advice.

"Excuse me miss? Could I get another whiskey? Actually, make it a double."

*   *   *

It wasn't long before the first catastrophic revelation was sprung on Bernie. Her father and stepmother picked her up from the airport. Thankfully, she was going to stay at Beth's for the duration of the trip (much easier than choosing between parental homes) but her father had wanted to pick her up. It was a 45-minute drive to Beth's apartment.

Confined to the back seat of her father's Cadillac, Bernie felt like a caged animal. She was restless from lack of sleep and too much booze on the plane. Her head was pounding, and while she could stretch out on the wide, soft leather seats in the back, she could not turn off her stepmother's voice. She had been speaking non-stop since they left the airport and now as they approached Beth's subdivision, her focus seemed strong. Her stepmother's voice would stay the course.

First, her stepmother started in on the state of small business today. As in: "So I said to the manicurist, you will fix my nails and do it for free because otherwise every single one of my friends will be hearing about it and when they do, they'll won't be coming here anymore. I mean, my God, Bernie! The woman couldn't tell the difference between Winter White polish and Pristine White. Can you believe that? Well, let me tell you – I could."

Then she set the world aright, focusing on the war in Iraq. "So I was like, thank God for the Iraq War because all those rich Arabs had to sell their properties. I'm talking serious real estate. I made an absolute bomb!"

The irony was lost on the woman. Not that she would have paused to conduct any close analysis of her own language.

Bernie had no chance. The woman could have crushed Saddam Hussain one handed.

As the car pulled off the expressway onto the exit ramp, her stepmother came out with her big announcement. She framed it excitedly, like it was a gift to be bestowed, whipping her head frequently around to catch Bernie's expression.

"So-o-o-o…" she began.

"Yeah?" Bernie responded.

"Now Bernadette, after we tell you this, just take some time and think about it. This is the kind of information you need a couple days to decide on."

Bernie waited, tensed for battle. She sensed trouble.

Her stepmother glanced at Bernie's father before twisting back, her right hand grasping the edge of her seat, with her head perched atop it. "So-o-o, Bernie, how does August 14th sound to you?"

"August 14th?"

"For the wedding."

"Sounds like a Monday," Bernie said.

"Yes, and… it could be your wedding day! Isn't that wonderful?" She hit Bernie's father's knee. "Tell her how wonderful it is!"

"It's wonderful," he said.

"A Monday?" Bernie didn't sound convinced.

"What! What's wrong with a Monday?" her stepmother said.

"People don't get married on Mondays."

"Sure they do!"

"They do?" Bernie was falling into that old trap of sounding interested. In weddings you never ask probing questions. Questions = Interest. Interest = Desire.

"Of course they do, just ask your father."

"Dad?" She caught his reflection in the rear-view mirror. She tried her best to look desperate.

"There is no law against it," he said.

"Well, that settles it!" Bernie cried out slapping the leather seat with her palm and sulking into a slouch. "If we won't get arrested, then of course we should do it!"

"Don't get smart with me, young lady!" he snapped.

"Dad, what do you expect! I know you want to save money but who will even come on a Monday? Oh, no. Is that why you did it? Is it so no one comes?"

"No, no. We want people to come. But it is cheaper. A lot cheaper," he confessed.

Bernie's stepmother turned to face her. Her eyes bore into Bernie's. Her lip liner was thinning away at the edges and trying to escape up the dry, microscopic lines that surrounded her lips. She bared her perfect white American teeth at her. "Bernie, your father is spending a lot of money on this wedding for you. It is your good fortune that we managed to call up and arrange this date for your wedding at all and you, my dear, should have just a little respect for that."

Bernie held her tongue. Within her stepmother's remarks was a more pertinent issue. "Did you just say you arranged the date already?"

"Well, who else will? Your mother? You in London? Your father has really gone out of his way for you and you are throwing it back in his face like a spoiled brat."

"Oh God…" Bernie's father sighed.

"Don't pull that 'God' crap on me. I've had enough! And if you aren't going to stick up for me, then I will. Your daughter is disrespecting everything we've ever done for her and you just ignore it."

"Look, we are pulling on to Beth's street now. Calm down."

Bernie's stepmother pouted in the passenger seat. The remaining journey was short, but she huffed from the front and shot killer eyes at Bernie through the vanity mirror. Bernie's dad pulled in to Beth's drive. When he stopped, she stomped out of the car and up the steps.

Beth swung the door open. Bernie heard a muffled complaint about her and then her stepmother disappeared into the house. Beth shrugged helplessly and followed.

Frozen in the car, neither Bernie nor her father spoke. He ran his hands up and down the steering wheel, finally turning off the radio and then the car altogether.

"Bernie," he said, "don't worry. It's all going to work out. People will still come. It doesn't matter what day it is, it's still going to be your big day."

"Except I don't get to choose the day."

"Compromises must be made. Come on, look at the position you're putting me in with your stepmother. Be fair."

"Dad, I haven't been allowed to make a single decision on this wedding. If I disagree, I'm disrespectful. If I have a different idea, I'm disrespectful. I'm not allowed to have an opinion on my own wedding."

"Now that's not true. We've made compromises too."

"Yes, to Mom. Meanwhile, I just have to go for whichever one of you wins the argument. Speaking of which, what's Mom think of this Monday situation?" The silence from the front seat was heavy and brooding. "I'm assuming you told her, right? Right?"

He glanced up at her through the rear-view mirror. "We thought you could tell her."

Bernie had a small stroke. "Me?"

"Yeah, well. It will be fine anyway. She's so cheap, she'll love it."

"Dad, she is never going to agree to a Monday wedding."

"But why not? If she wants to pay more money for it to be on a weekend, fine. She can pay for it. She took the house, she is not going to hijack this wedding."

This is a conversation that may sound familiar to those traversing the delicate path of the divorced couple. "Bernadette," he continued, "I've spent your whole life making compromises to that woman, and I've decided this is where I'm putting my foot down."

What was Bernie to say when she heard this? Weddings are the epitome of compromise. The ceremony embodies compromise. Bernie's Aunt Angie had already insisted on a front row seat and she would get it even though she hadn't made a family appearance in years. At the reception, vegans would be catered to. The seating plan alone would need UN-style negotiations.

"Dad," she said, trying to hide the terror in her voice, "Dad I just think that perhaps my wedding may not be the time for getting back at her."

"That's what you think," he said.

This lifelong resentment between her father and mother was one Bernie thought had been laid to rest long ago.

But then, Bernie had thought that her relationship with her parents had hit a new level of understanding and maturity. That alone shows us how little Bernie had prepared herself for what was to come.

*   *   *

Being cocooned in Beth's home did not isolate Bernie from endless negotiations. After relieving herself of her father and stepmother the night before, the following morning Bernie's mother picked her up bright and early. Bernie was still wiping the sleep from her eyes when the doorbell rang and her mother swept into her room.

"Rise and shine," her mother sang, "sing out the glory, glory!" She pulled the blind and it rattled upward. "It's a bea-u-tiful day."

"You're chipper this morning," Bernie grumbled.

Her mother plopped herself down on the side of the bed. "That's because my baby is back." Bernie smiled. She loved her mother when she was like this. She had energy and sparkle. She made it seem as if anything – even her stepmother's grand plan – could be set aright.

Bernie shifted up from under the blankets. Her mother brushed the hair from her eyes. "Now there's my beautiful girl," she said softly. She gave Bernie a quick hug and kiss and patted her on her head. "Right. Up and at 'em. We've got places to go and people to meet!"

Bernie changed quickly. This welcome from her mother suddenly made her feel optimistic, even in light of the conversation with her father last night. She bounded into the car, but she did not, however, mention any of yesterday's conversation while in the car. Even though the drive to a possible wedding venue took over an hour, Bernie didn't find one of those minutes appropriate to introduce a Monday wedding. At the same time, since she wasn't paying for it, and since her mother wasn't paying for it, she felt she had no choice but to bow to her father's wishes. She reminded herself that marrying Sam, not having a big weekend bash, was the objective.

In the long stretch of road leading up to the venue, weaving through the hills and forests of Southeast Michigan, Bernie stayed silent. She rationalised this by reflecting on the rarity of their common vision. Her mother hated grey-panelled, windowless rooms as much as she did.

On the return journey, they stopped for a bite to eat at an old favourite of theirs off Woodward Avenue. Bernie indulged in her first American meal by ordering all that was absent from her culinary life in London.

"I'll have a side salad," she began, "with Ranch dressing, then the Club sandwich and a bowl of clam chowder. Thank you."

The waiter turned to her mother, but her eyes were on her daughter. "Bernadette… don't you think that is a lot of food?"

"Yes, but I don't get to eat like this in London."

"Well, I'm sorry to say Bernadette, but you don't get to eat like that and fit into a wedding dress either."

"Mother, please. Just order."

"I am your mother, honey, it is my job to help you."

"Mother…"

Her mother's lips pursed, ready to start again but instead she relaxed. "Okay. I'll have the grilled chicken salad but I'll pass on the Creamy Italian dressing. Could I just have oil and vinegar on the side to mix myself? No olives, no onions and no cheese."

The menus were whisked away, and in their absence Bernie could feel her mother's thoughts attempting to penetrate her brain. "Bernadette," she said, "I sense there is something you aren't telling me."

"No," she said too quickly.

Her mother's eyes probed her. It was uncomfortable. Mothers can see all. "Bernadette…"

The effort of keeping this information inside her for hours and then being undone by her mother in less than thirty seconds was exhausting. She reached for her water and shifted nervously. "Oh, fine! It's Dad. He wants to have the wedding on a Monday."

"A Monday!" her mother huffed. "This is news to me. Oh, Bernadette, what have you done?"

"It's not me, it's them."

"This is just like your father. He isn't thinking about you, he's thinking about his wallet."

"Not surprisingly, as he is paying for most of it."

"He is not. I am buying your dress."

"You are? You never mentioned it." This was a revelation to Bernie. She was stunned and touched at the unexpected offer, even if it was small potatoes compared with the rest of the wedding.

"Don't be silly, Bernadette," her mother said rolling her eyes, "Of course I did. But in any case, as far as the rest of it goes, your father should pay for most of it. He has the money to, and, more importantly, it's tradition."

Tradition was her mother's escape from modern responsibilities. When it concerned her finances, tradition was an oft-played card.

"I know how to solve this," her mother continued with a self-satisfied grin. "Tell your father we will help out a bit. But tell him, I will not contribute at all if my daughter's perfect day is on a Monday." She reached across the table and squeezed Bernie's hand. "That is just not perfect."

Bernie should have been pleased. It was a stunning offer of generosity from her mother. Instead she recognised an old feeling revisiting her. It was claustrophobia. She had officially returned to her childhood role of divorcee-go-between. It was a tight fit. She tried one desperate shot at appeasing her mother so her parents would speak to each other instead of through her.

"Of course, if you wanted to help out financially, it would cost less and you'd get a greater say if I did get married on a Monday. You could call Dad yourself and make the offer."

"You mean because my money would go further and influence more because everything we'd hire would be cheaper that day?"

"Yes, but other things too. The bar bill would be cheaper for one. People won't drink nearly as much on a Monday."

"Bernadette, don't be ridiculous," her mother said simply as she placed her napkin in her lap. "That isn't going to be a problem anyway."

"Why not?"

"Because there isn't going to be any alcohol at this wedding."

So much for common ground. From where Bernie sat, the ground was looking pretty shaky.

Wedding Truth No. 10

When you start getting what you want – shut up. Resist temptation to argue.

This is so difficult. Arguing comes so easy to family members. I, for one, am totally incapable of keeping my mouth shut.

After waiting weeks to hear my mother say it, now I had confirmation. She wanted to take part in planning my wedding. I was on the cusp of attaining my dream wedding yet again. Like most daughters, I still craved my mother's approval. Her involvement in the wedding equalled that to me.

The temptation to stop her mid conversation and insist on an open bar for my guests was practically irresistible. Even after she offered financial assistance towards the wedding, and my dress! But this meant we would go shopping together – the ultimate in female bonding, shopping for the ultimate in female attire.

But in the back of my mind, I knew I had a lot of explaining to do, not the least of which to my fiancé and his father, who both, in the traditional Welsh definition of it, saw a wedding as a drinking occasion. And it seemed to have escaped my mother's attention that, besides flying over for it, his parents were contributing financially to the wedding as well.

Again, I managed to keep my mouth shut and hope for the best. We all know how well that strategy had worked so far.

Chapter Ten: The Dry Wedding, Or "Beer Is Just Not Civil"

When Bernie called Sam on the phone from Detroit, he sounded frantic for the first time in the lead up to the wedding.

"No alcohol?" he said, voice cracking.

"None," Bernie replied.

"Not wine? Not champagne?"

Bernie wanted to be reassuring, but her parents were irrational people. "Apparently we are allowed a champagne toast but no one else will be partaking." That in itself had been a 15-minute debate. Bernie shuddered to think how long the negotiations would last in order for every guest to toast the wedding.

It wasn't that her family didn't drink. Even her mother had the odd glass of wine with dinner. But alcohol consumption was always done in strict moderation. Her mother, it seemed, did not trust the rest of the guests to stick to her ideas of moderation. The first rule of which was: one glass is plenty, two is too many.

"How am I supposed to explain that to my father? How am I supposed to say to him, to my brother, to my friends, 'Thanks for flying half-way around the world, but I can't possibly offer you a pint?' How?" Sam was teetering on total hysteria.

"Sam, I don't know. I am trying."

"Try harder!"

"I am. I spent the whole of the meal trying to turn my mother around but she will have none of it. I thought she was just trying to save money so I said we could just have wine and beer."

"And…"

"And she looked at me horrified and asked if I planned on my guests walking around with plastic cups, filling them up at the keg in the corner. She asked if I was having a wedding or a fraternity party."

The second rule of alcohol: sipping wine is elegant, slugging beer is nasty.

"Tell her it's a fraternity party! Tell her anything!"

"Calm down. I'm seeing my father later today. Surely he won't agree with this plan."

*   *   *

Stretched out across the backseat of her father's car the next day, Bernie devoted herself entirely to the beverage crisis. On the outside she appeared mild mannered, but a closer inspection would make obvious the pressure she was feeling. She shifted uncomfortably on the luxurious upholstery, realigning her clothes and picking at her nails.

In her head tumbled everyone's opinions, none of them her own. Monday wedding, dividing the costs, dry reception, beer as a necessity. Weighing against all this was Bernie's fantasy wedding. It was the same one applauded in all the wedding magazines and guidebooks she read. The one where her family beamed proudly from their pew as she walked down the aisle. The one where her father shook Sam's hand and welcomed him into the family. The one where she was the glowing bride surrounded by everyone she loved while they raised their glasses to the best man's toast.

What relation did that fantasy have to the beer brawl her mother envisioned? The ridiculous Monday wedding? The war room negotiations between her mother and father?

The further the plans were from the ideal wedding, the more desperately Bernie wanted it. She felt cheated. Why did all of popular culture seem to agree that weddings are blissful, harmonious occasions?

If it was meant to be her big day, why did she feel so selfish asking for her guests to be entertained on a weekend or allowed to have a drink at the reception? Where were the guides with chapters called: "When Parents Attack – How to deal with the immature antics of the most important adults in your life"?

She gave up. Bliss it wasn't.

Up front, her father and stepmother were arguing over the fastest way to get to the deli for brunch.

"If you take Orchard Lake Road," she said, "we will get stuck in traffic and never, ever get there."

"It will be fine."

"Fine! Right. If you don't take Farmington and then go over, we will be eating our brunch at lunch."

"I drive this way every day. It will be fine."

"Dad," Bernie blurted out from the back. "Mom wants a weekend wedding and she says if you do this, she'll be willing to help more money wise, but she doesn't want any alcohol at the wedding, but Sam does and I don't know what to tell him, what do you think?"

"Breathe lately?" he said in return.

"Dad!"

"Hey, if your mother wants to help more, great! I'm not saying she will, because we all know she won't, but if this might squeeze out a couple of dollars from her, then fine – Sunday it is."

"Sunday?"

"Oh, and I suppose Sunday is no good for you either?" her stepmother said curtly.

"No! No, much better. Ideal really. No problem. Sunday, sounds great."

Her stepmother grimaced. "See, finally some sense."

"What about the alcohol though?"

Her stepmother looked up at her through her vanity mirror. "Well, for once, I agree with your mother. No alcohol is the way to go. I'm not going to have beer sloshing all over the venue, smelling up the place."

"But it wouldn't be like that."

"Oh, it wouldn't, would it? I can just imagine it now. Red plastic cups, like at the basketball game. People puking in the corners. Is that the classy affair you want as a bride?"

Bernie was perplexed. How could she argue against this? It wasn't as if she wanted people puking in corners either. She tried nevertheless. "It's not just about me. It's Sam's wedding too and he wants to share a beer with his father at the reception. Who are we to deny them that?"

"Bernadette," her stepmother stated, "We have a lot of people coming to this wedding. Your father is inviting his boss. I am inviting my closest friends. This is an important event for us all. We can't have people acting like it is a sporting event. You know what happens when people start drinking: riots. That's what happens. Riots."

Bernie slumped over in the backseat. It was worse than she thought. It wasn't just a wedding anymore, it was a social event. A networking opportunity for her father's business. Money wasn't an issue at all. Social standards needed to be upheld.

"So what do you propose I tell Sam then? No, you can't have a beer with your father? No, you can't offer a drink to your best man who has spent loads of money and flown thousands of miles to be there. No, sorry."

There was silence from the front seat. Her father looked to her stepmother for an answer to this dilemma. For her stepmother's part, she was focusing on fixing her lip liner.

"You know what, Bernadette," she said, snapping her mirror closed. "You tell Sam, he can have his beer with his father and best man. But, and this is a big but, they will have to drink it away from the guests. Okay?" She turned to face Bernadette in the backseat, reached over and squeezed her hand. She smiled generously. "We aren't unreasonable people."

"Absolutely," her father said with enthusiasm, obviously pleased that a consensus had been arranged. "I may even join them." A quick glare from Bernie's stepmother put a stop to that.

Puritans they were not. Religious they were not. Bernie herself had seen them drink. Okay, it was Manischewitz and the odd Bloody Mary, but still alcohol had passed their lips.

Bernie just shook her head and tried not to cry. When had her family become so narrow-minded?

Wedding Truth No. 11

Sometimes compromise means you agree to everything they want.

At some point whilst planning a wedding, every bride takes a good hard look around her and realises that her wedding has been hijacked. She is meant to feel grateful for this. As in: "Look what we bought you for your wedding! 26-inch high, clear pink plastic swans to place on everyone's plates and matching plaid chair covers! Don't worry about the cost – we'll pay for them all."

In between conversations with my mother about what type of non-alcoholic cocktails my guests preferred, my stepmother was meeting me for endless visits to golf courses and hotel banqueting halls. The wedding in my mind was set outside in summer gardens, followed by drinks and food at dusk with friends, inside a room with high ceilings, wooden floors and candles.

Instead, I saw plenty of wood panelling but it was on the walls. The rooms were dark and windowless. The gardens were landscaped, but so are all putting greens.

One thing about the venues did stand out. Most of these places may have catered more to sales conventions than weddings, but one factor united them all. Every single one of them had a bar, sometimes two or three. How was it their participants were allowed to celebrate a little but mine weren't? What did it say about what my family thought of my wedding that they weren't all that interested in the guests honouring it with a toast?

Chapter Eleven: The Wedding Barn

As a teenager, and arguably long after, Bernie embodied very few of the ideals of feminine beauty. Tomboy or grunge would have been a more accurate description.

In the course of her transformation from teenage scruff to professional bride, Bernie wore up to five piercings in various locations, four hair colours, hundreds of hair cuts, almost zero make up and at one point, coincidentally the same period she met Sam, her wardrobe consisted of two pairs of jeans, four t-shirts, four pairs of knickers, three pairs of socks, one hoodie and no bras.

The day that Sam introduced her to his mum, back when they were still at university together, Bernie adorned herself in ripped jeans, spiky hair and a tongue piercing. To her great credit and character, Sam's mum managed to overlook these accoutrements and welcome Bernie into her home. Sam's father was there for the introduction as well, although really only in a physical sense. As opposed to Sam's mother, his father made more of an impression on Bernie than she did on him. When she walked in, ripped jeans and all, into his backroom to introduce herself, she found him in the middle of the Welsh National Anthem, standing, voice ringing out, tears in his eyes. Wales v Ireland was his only concern. Bernie was just a tiny blip on the menu that day.

If you were Bernie's mother, or Sam's even, in your wildest dreams would this pierced, grungy girl have even the remotest chance of evolving into a princess bride?

And yet, once she was engaged, the dress – in all its puritanical white, lacy, splendidness – became an absolute obsession for Bernie. Why? Put it down to that moment when all teenage rebellion falls flat, love rules and a girl just wants to be pretty.

Until her mother's offer, Bernie had no hope of achieving this fairytale moment. Now, despite it amounting to the down-payment on a house, the dress was going to be hers. It was no wonder that she didn't press the whole no-alcohol issue immediately.

For her mother, this must have been a dream moment after all those years of watching her daughter slum it in horrible flannel t-shirts and ripped baggy jeans. She remembered a sweet little girl who loved to have her hair curled into long ringlets and refused to wear a dress unless it was adorned with a wide satin bow and designed to hit a certain altitude when twirled. That girl was back.

Equally excited, Beth could barely control herself when she learned that Bernie would be dress shopping. She cornered Bernie while she was brushing her hair in the bathroom on the morning that her mother was coming to take her shopping.

Beth said, "You do realise if you buy a dress, you will be wearing one, right? Right?"

Bernie acted as if this was totally normal behaviour. "I have worn dresses before you know."

"Like this? Big? White? Fluffy like a cotton ball? Sparkling with beads?"

Bernie rolled her eyes at her sister's reflection. "I'm not going to look like a snowman."

"No, you'll look like a snowwoman."

"It will be fine," Bernie put the brush down on the counter. She was having difficulty verbalising her desire for a wedding dress, which even she felt was not in her nature. "I, um, I want one."

This broke Beth completely into a fit of giggles. Then she looked up. "Oh my God. You're serious aren't you?"

Bernie nodded. "I'm not the same girl I was five years ago. I've grown up. I want to feel grown up."

Beth squealed with glee. Beth was a very girlie girl. She loved dressing up. Unlike Bernie's ten item wardrobe of the 1990s, Beth had amassed more like ten wardrobes. "In that case," she said, "I am coming!" She ran from the room to get dressed.

Not long after, Bernie's mother arrived at the house. She seemed pleased to have Beth along for the ride. "All the girls together again," she said clapping her hands lightly. She hugged Bernie briefly and then pulled away. Her displeasure at Bernie's attire was obvious. "Bernadette," she said looking her up and down, "do you think that jeans are appropriate for this type of shopping?"

As usual when her mother asked her such questions, Bernie felt totally ill at ease and perplexed. Where was her mother planning on taking her? What kind of wedding gown boutique didn't accept women in jeans who were willing to pay big money? She looked down at her dirty trainers and backed down immediately. "I'll go change," she said. She went back into the bedroom she was using at her sister's and changed into a long skirt and heels like her mother. She felt uncomfortable, but then she *was* about to purchase the most expensive outfit she would ever wear in her life; maybe her mother was right, and some clothes befitting the occasion were necessary.

On the long ride to the shop, Beth chatted non stop to both of them about the wedding dress clippings she'd taken from the magazines since she was nine, now littering the backseat of the car where she sat.

Beth grabbed one and thrust it around the passenger seat into Bernie's face. "This would totally suit your figure, Bernadette. A-line. Don't you agree Mom? Maybe with a sweeping bow across the front?"

"I thought something simple," her mother responded. "Bernadette won't want anything too ostentatious."

Bernie had no idea what she wanted. She didn't know an A-line from a B-line – though incidentally a bee-line was what she wanted to do more than anything right now. A bee-line out the moving car. What was she thinking? She hated shopping!

"There will be food at some point today, right?" she asked her mother hopefully.

"Oh, Bernadette!" her mother said, breaking into fits of giggles. She swapped her gaze to Beth via the rear-view mirror. "Beth, isn't this just like when we used to go shopping when you were kids?"

Beth laughed, "Yeah, totally!"

"Don't worry honey," her mother continued, "you'll get some ice cream later. A little reward." More giggling.

For some reason, this made Bernie feel better, even though they were teasing her. She looked out the window wistfully. The Michigan countryside shone in the cold spring morning as they drove west out of the suburbs. Bernie allowed herself a quick daydream in which her wedding day was just as beautiful, blossoms everywhere, sun shining, clear sapphire blue skies, enormous lakes... Lakes? Where were they? She whipped her head around just catching the sign for Kennsington National Park.

"Mom? Mom, where are we going?"

"Fowlerville."

"Fowlerville? That's miles away. Why there? There are plenty of wedding boutiques around us."

"My friend Carol, you know the seamstress? She told me about this place. You'll love it. She said if we found anything we liked, she'd help us make changes. And I'm sure she'll do the changes for free."

Bernie always worried when anyone told her she'd love something, especially in regards to the wedding. It always seemed to end with her being corralled into something she hated. She slunk lower in her seat and hoped that Fowlerville contained more than the one drugstore and gas station she remembered from passing it on the way to visit friends at university five years ago.

Forty minutes later her mother pulled off the highway and on to a long country road. It stretched as far as she could see with hilly peaks and crevices. Her mother turned right. "Mom? Fowlerville is left."

"Oh I know," she assured Bernadette, "I'm headed the opposite way."

Bernie stared at the opposite. She saw nothing. No towns. No stores. Certainly no wedding boutiques. "Mom? Where is this place? There is nothing here."

Beth piped in from the back. "Mom, we're in the middle of

nowhere. Are you sure you know where you are headed?"

"Of course I do." She sounded confident. They'd have to trust her. Bernie turned to flash an anxious look at her sister, but Beth was already reimmersed in wedding dress magazines.

The road stretched on for miles with no civilization in sight. America is like that. Remove yourself from a big city in any state and it's like insta-country. Michigan is no different.

Her mother hummed lightly to herself, glancing down every once in a while at the directions on her lap. "Oh! There it is," she suddenly cried out swerving the car slightly.

Beth craned her torso through to the front seats. "Where?" she asked.

"There." Her mother pointed. In the distance, at a crossroads about a half-mile away, was a farm.

"Mom, that's a farm," Beth said.

"No, that's where my daughter is going to find her wedding dress."

Bernie couldn't help herself. "In a barn? I'm going to find my dress in a barn?" Her voice broke anxiously.

They were closer now. Close enough to see the large, white, sparkling letters surrounded by neon, blinking lights: 'Gigi's Wedding Land'. And in smaller but no less subtle colourings: 'XXX-Large to XXX-Small, come on in, we got 'em all!'

Bernie's mother pulled up the dirt road and into Gigi's parking lot. Neither Beth nor Bernie had spoken since they laid eyes on the barn. Bernie struggled to keep her profound aversion hidden as she opened the car door and placed one foot after the other. She watched her feet move towards the entrance.

The two automatic doors swung inwards like the entrance to some old-town western saloon. They were greeted by a surly, teenage salesgirl. "Welcome to Gigi's Wedding Land," she said in an absolute monotone. "When others can't make your dream come true, look to us and we'll help you. If other stores have turned you away, fear not, today's your dream day." She paused to scratch her ear and chomp on her gum. "My name's Melinda. How can I make your dream come true?"

Even Bernie's mother seemed perplexed. "Um," she said. "Um."

"Mom?" Beth saw clearly her mother's difficulty trying to communicate with a snotty teenager. "Look Melinda, maybe you can just point us in the right direction and we'll find you if we need anything."

Melinda shrugged. "Okay. If you head straight ahead you will find our reconditioned dresses from size 0 – 22. Up the stairs to the right are our new dresses, in sample sizes. And then it's up the ladders to get any of the specialised gear like veils and shoes and stuff. But, like, a lot of people don't like climbing the ladder so if you want, I can do that for you."

Beth grabbed Bernie's arm and pulled her towards the new dresses on the right. "Thanks Melinda," she called back. Melinda squatted back down on her stool and started playing with her chewing gum.

Their mother called to them. "I'm going to go look at the reconditioned dresses. Maybe I can find you a deal, okay Bernadette?"

Bernie mumbled a response. She moved on autopilot now, following Beth as she rummaged through the endless racks of white crinoline wrapped in clear plastic protective covers.

Besides herself, everyone else in the store seemed oblivious to the tacky aura of desperation in the shop. The place was packed out with women clawing their way to a bargain. Beth kept pulling out dresses and asking Bernie what she thought, but Bernie just shrugged.

"You're trying on one of these whether you like it or not," Beth pointed out just at the moment their mother reappeared with three dresses draped across her arm.

"Bernadette, why don't you start with these?" she said. Bernie rolled her eyes.

Beth grabbed them and pushed Bernie towards the dressing room. Bernie fell inside. She plopped on a stool. Beth glanced back at their mother, now rifling through the new dress racks. She shut the door so just she and Bernie were locked inside.

"What are you doing?" Beth whispered shrilly.

Bernie broke into tears. "Beth," she sobbed, "I thought I was going to wear the most beautiful dress. I thought it was all going to be so perfect. But now I'm in the wedding barn and I'm going to walk down the aisle in some big, puffy monstrosity. And it won't even be mine! It will be a pre-owned model." She sniffed and wiped her eyes on her sleeve.

There was a knock on the door. "How's our bride?" It was their mother. Bernie didn't answer.

"Fine, Mom," Beth said. She pulled a dress from the stack and cracked open the door. "Mom, can you see if they have this one in white? This is ivory."

"No problem, back in a moment."

Bernie slumped in her stool with her head down, wiped more tears from her cheek and waited for Beth's consoling voice. It didn't come. She looked up. Beth had her arms crossed and was staring at her sternly.

She said, "What are you doing, Bernadette?"

"Crying?" Bernie offered.

"You are such a baby. Get a grip! Okay, we're in a wedding barn and yes it's pretty terrible, but it's a start. A week ago you didn't even have a dress, now you have an opportunity to get one for free!"

Bernie caught her reflection in the mirror. She did look a bit pathetic.

Beth continued, "And you know Mom would never make you wear some dress you hated. She wants you to look gorgeous and she is excited about buying this for you. Give her a chance!" Beth reached into her bag and pulled out a tissue. "Now, wipe your eyes and let's get you into one of these beautiful creations."

Bernie shrugged off her snobby attitude. She shrugged off her clothes as well. Beth helped her into the first dress. It had a hoop skirt underneath so large and stiff it could dam up a river. The sleeves resembled those inflatable safety rings parents put on children's arms in pools, except these were faux-satin and pristine white. The corset pushed her breasts to her chin.

Turning around to her sister, Bernie said, "Beth, look – I'm going to be the first bride who dies on her wedding night due to suffocation by her own breasts."

"At least you have boobs," Beth sighed with longing.

"I heard that," their mother said. "You both are perfect, now come on out and let me see."

Beth swung the door open at her command. Bernie tried to keep a straight face, but failed. Even their mother laughed. "Well you certainly fill it out," she said.

"Mother!" both Bernie and Beth shouted.

"But you know," Bernie could see her mother imagining a tuck here, a bit of material there, "if we went to Carol and had her take a look, she might be able to let it out a bit around the chest and shorten it." She looked at the price tag. "It could work."

"No way, Mother," Bernie said.

"No way," Beth agreed.

"Okay, okay. I can take a hint. Are there any others? I tried to find some more, but I don't see anything that I really feel is appropriate."

"Does that mean we can go home?" Bernie said hopefully.

"No, but it does mean we have enough time to check out some places near us. Remember Bernie, you are leaving in a few days. Today's all we have."

Bernie thought, *Then maybe we shouldn't have wasted it driving all the way out here?* At least she had the decency to remember Beth's admonishing talk earlier and not vocalise it.

Bernie yanked up the skirt and scratched her leg under all the layers. "Agh!" she said, "Beth, I'm itching like mad. Get it off me!"

"Calm down, woman, I'll help you out of the thing." Their mother shut the door politely while Beth yanked the dress up and over Bernie's head. As soon as it was off, Bernie began attacking her itching skin.

"Oh, God. Bernie!" Beth was holding the dress and staring at her.

"What?" Bernie said, reaching around her back to scratch at a shoulder blade. Beth turned her slowly to face the mirror. From top to bottom, wherever the dress had touched her, Bernie was covered in a swollen, red rash.

Bernie's eyes and mouth fell.

"Mom!" Beth cried out. "Mom, come quick!"

Their mother stormed into the room. "What is it?"

"Mom, look at Bernie."

"Mom, I'm dying!" Bernie said.

"Oh goodness. Don't exaggerate Bernadette. Your skin has always been sensitive. I'll just get some wet paper towels. We'll wipe you down and you'll be fine." She left.

Bernadette slumped back on to the stool. "Beth," she said, "I'm allergic."

"Only to one crappy dress."

"No, to getting married."

Wedding Truth No. 12

Wedding dress shopping is an exercise in humiliation.

Shopping for a wedding dress bears no relation to normal shopping. Forget what you've been told; it's not a pampering, beauty-affirming experience. Nothing close.

At wedding boutiques, the salesgirls are intimidating and only seen with appointments. They look you up and down, judging the size of your ass as well as your wallet as soon as you walk in the door. The dresses are enormous in every way. Too difficult to negotiate without assistance, you're forced to get naked and allow salesgirls to touch you. And they are enormously expensive. For the price of an entirely new wardrobe, you pay for a dress you will only wear once. Soul destroying.

Normally, a customer tries on items according to size. This is totally reasonable. In wedding stores, regardless of size, the bride tries on everything in either a size 8 or 10. Of course, most women are not a size 10, let alone an 8. No worries there, ladies: all shops come equipped with enormous, back-length, fluorescent pink banana clips to hold the dress together when it won't zip. How thoughtful.

I was very lucky. I fit into sample sizes. My first secret: I'm a short-ass. Second: The wedding diet. All brides go on it. Two parts stress to one part fluorescent clips. Clips are very motivational.

This meant that when I found a dress I loved (which I did), I could buy the sample off the rack for half price. The saleswoman tried to convince my mother that we should buy a pristine new one because the bottom of the sample dresses become dirty after hundreds of brides trample over them. My mother assured the woman that I was so short, they'd have to hem off half the dress anyway. The dress was mine: Joy!

Chapter Twelve: When Parents Attack

The shrill blaring of the phone woke Bernie with a start. She cracked her eyelids open and shuddered. "Ugh," she moaned, caveman-style, throwing a pillow over her head. Today was the day. She was probably already late for it. She cheered silently at this realisation.

Today her family would be meeting in the ultimate showdown before she returned to London: parent v. parent; mother v. stepmother; one kitchen table, one daughter caught in the crossfire.

With a pillow over her head, Bernie assured herself that she would not have to get up. Then the door cracked open and Beth bobbed in.

"Guess who that was on the phone?" Beth's voice was cotton candy, sugary-sweet.

"Leave me alone. I'm sleeping 'til tomorrow," Bernie answered. She peeked her head momentarily out from under the pillow. Beth smiled at her. No, a second glance revealed she was actually smirking.

"It was Mom," Beth said. "She doesn't want you to be late. That would be terrible, wouldn't it?" Beth emphasised "terrible" with a small giggle.

"You're enjoying this!" Bernie said.

"No. No, I'm not." Beth shook her head vigorously. A bit too vigorously for Bernie's taste.

"Yes, you are!"

Beth plopped herself on the edge of the bed. "Are you kidding? Of course I am! This is great for me."

"For you?" Bernie snarled at her. "I have no idea what you mean. But whatever it is, I don't like it."

This didn't faze her sister, who continued with a huge, satisfied grin. "No, just imagine, Bernadette. I am finally the good daughter. After all these years, you're older, you always got to stay out later, your grades were always higher, – "

"Yeah. My 'A' in English Lit is really doing me a lot of good now."

Beth smacked her hand down on her knee. "My point exactly. It won't help you at all today. On the other hand, the deeper you dig this hole, the better I look. I'm thinking of admitting to all kinds of faults tonight once this is over. Like how I spent way too much on clothes and crap this month. I need to ask Dad for a loan to make my rent. A few hundred dollars is small potatoes compared to this money pit."

Bernie made an attempt to arrange more pillows over her head and sink deeper under the covers. "Wake me up tomorrow."

"No way. Get up. Get moving. The shower's all yours." On her way out, Beth pulled all the bedding off her.

Bernie shouted at her, "You know, I'm more than this wedding! I have a real life and deal with real things as well!"

Beth popped her head back in though the doorway. "Not from my point of view. I'm going to milk this for all it's worth." Her voice trailed off into fits of giggles. "I'll put coffee on. You need your energy to maintain this level of mayhem."

Finally, Bernie relented and clambered into the shower. Like many times during the wedding planning, she wondered how she had reached this terrible situation. Who was she kidding? Her mother and stepmother couldn't agree to anything. It was bound to be a total disaster.

Yesterday, her father had seemed optimistic. "Ask your mother to meet up," he said. Actually, now that she thought about it, he seemed more resigned to his fate than optimistic. "Tell her we'll discuss it. The wedding."

"You could call her yourself," Bernie suggested.

His voice rose perceptively. "Why would I do that? It's your wedding. Besides, you think I want to talk to your mother that bad, I'd call her?"

Bernie couldn't win. Her father acted like he was doing her a favour by asking her to arrange her own execution. While she scrubbed her hair, she fantasised about grabbing a shovel from Beth's garage and digging her own grave with it.

Bernie turned off the shower as Beth banged on the door. "Hurry up!" she called. "Anne's here to pick you up. I know you don't want to be late." More laughter.

Bernie imagined jumping into the grave to hide, but instead she just towelled off and dressed.

She grabbed her bag and coat and ran from the house before Beth could say anything else. Behind her the screen-door banged shut. She leapt into the car.

"What's got into you? You're not actually looking forward to this, are you?" One glance from Bernie confirmed the total opposite. Unfortunately for Bernie, Anne found her attitude as amusing as Beth had.

The whole ride, Anne kept breaking into fits of giggles. "I'm sorry. This is just so entertaining."

Bernie crossed her arms and murmured glumly, "Yeah. Ha-ha. I just got all this from my sister. What a support network."

"Oh, stop sulking, Bern!" Anne reached across and scuffed up her hair. "You have to admit this is pure comedy. I wish I was going."

Bernie brightened. "You could, you know. I know people. I could get you a great seat. Front row."

"No way! And risk being hit by a flying plate?" More giggles from the driver.

Bernie picked at her seat-belt, pulling it back and forth, hoping for an accident. "Aim for a truck," she said. This request only produced more laughter. Not long after, Anne pulled up at the house.

"This is it, kid-o. The end of the line."

Bernie sat, totally unfazed, pretending they were at a red light. She avoided Anne's stare and focused on a tree. Anne reached across her and pulled on the door handle. The car door swung open with a great thud.

"Meet you for a couple of beers later?" Anne offered.

"If I'm alive," Bernie moaned and got out.

In a Western movie, her parents would've met behind swinging barroom doors while bushels of straw blew listlessly across the barren road outside. The meeting was scheduled for high noon, but instead of whiskey and gunslingers, Bernie's mother had prepared her best silver, shined and set. Tea was ready in the pot along with two pints of coffee, caffeinated and de-caffeinated. A decanter of freshly squeezed orange juice nestled between a basket of warm, sliced bagels and a crystal bowl of fresh fruit. Cooling on top of silver trays covered with white paper doilies, were home made cookies and slices of coffee cake.

Bernie sat in the kitchen while her mother waltzed across the room fixing items and replacing others. At the crackling of a car up the driveway, Bernie jumped to the door. Her mother followed, removing her apron first, then pressing down her hair and shirt with her hands as she walked.

"Good afternoon," her mother said, a smile creasing her face as she opened the door.

"Yeah. Hi." Bernie's father returned curtly. He reached over and pecked Bernie on the cheek. "And hi to you too, sweetie." He clapped his hands. "Right, when do we start?"

"Dad?" Bernie asked.

"What?"

Bernie pointed to the screen door. Its outline framed her stepmother. Her fuchsia and silver-striped sweater was tucked firmly into her white trousers, a belt cinched her waist. Her arms were crossed and she stared at Bernie's father over her glasses. "So!" she called out. "Are you going to open this or what?"

Bernie's father grabbed the door and swung it open. He apologised as she stormed in.

Ever the gracious host, Bernie's mother ignored this. She guided them into the kitchen and her grand buffet. Bernie's stepfather was already tucking in. "Oh," he mumbled, his mouth full of coffee cake. He directed them to sit down.

Bernie's father pulled out a chair for his wife. She sat down gingerly, perching on the edge of her seat, mouth down-turned. Her father slumped into his. He considered a pastry but pulled his hand back.

"Go ahead," Bernie's mother said encouragingly. But Bernie's father caught his wife's expression and thought the better.

"Nah, let's just start these negotiations. And pass the coffee." He paused. "De-caf." Bernie's mother reached over and poured coffee into a china cup for him. The cup clinked sweetly in the saucer as she lifted it to place in front of him.

All this time, Bernie sat in total silence. She didn't eat. She didn't drink. She didn't say anything. This is how she meant to remain for the meeting.

"Now, Bernadette tells me that you want to put in some money. Is that true?" her father started.

"Yes. That is true. We'd…"

He interrupted her. "Well, the way I see it, we have a lot more guests than you. If we split the costs by the percentage of guests, that seems fair to us." Bernie thought this was very reasonable, not that she would say so. She remained cowed, curled in her seat awaiting complete mayhem.

Therefore, it didn't surprise Bernie in the slightest when her mother questioned this offer. "And who will cover Bernadette and Sam's guests?" her mother inquired.

"Well, we'll split them 50/50."

Bernie's mother and stepfather exchanged knowing glances. "The thing is," Bernie's stepfather started, "we have calculated the prices for every item of the wedding. Your idea sounds reasonable, but I think when you look at how we've divided it, the cost percentage probably amounts to approximately the same."

What did they mean? Bernie struggled to remember discussing any costs of anything with either side. Or maybe it wasn't important to discuss costs with her because she was just supposed to go along with everything.

Her stepfather slid a printed list across the kitchen table to her father. He flipped it over and scanned the page. "I see," he said, relaying the information to the group, "so you feel that by paying for the flowers and decorations, cake, wedding dress and guest gifts that you will cover your share?"

Next to her father, Bernie's stepmother turned a scarlet-red. Her cheeks swelled with fury. Her manicured nails scratched against the tabletop. "What is this?" she spat.

"I think you will find it works out very fairly," her stepfather added.

"I know what this is," her stepmother said, ignoring him. "I know! You want to buy all the pretty things! You don't want us to have any say on how the wedding looks. You aren't interested in our opinions. You think we have bad taste!"

Bernie looked to her mother. Her expression was transparent and defiant. It was true. Her mother didn't want her father or stepmother to have a vote about anything on show to the guests. She wanted the credit and look of the wedding to be all her own. Bernie took a deep breath. This was going to get messy.

Her stepmother turned to her father. "Are you going to let them offend us like that? Are you going to let this happen? I would've gone and picked out things with them. Why won't they do the same for us?"

Her father turned away. "Wait a minute. Let's hear them out," he said.

"Hear them out! If you won't stick up for us, I'm not hanging around to get shit on! I'll be in the car." Her chair scrapped back against the linoleum floor and she disappeared.

The room was silent. Bernie's father reached for a cookie. He stuffed it in his mouth in one bite. Then he pointed a finger to his coffee cup. "Throw some caffeinated in here," he mumbled, a few crumbs shooting from his mouth. Bernie's mother delicately lifted the silver coffeepot and poured some into his cup.

Bernie's stepfather finally spoke. "We aren't trying to offend either of you, obviously."

"Obviously," her father repeated in between slurps from his coffee.

Her stepfather continued, "I think we all know whose day this is though. And frankly, it isn't ours."

Bernie was shocked. Did she hear correctly? Was someone at the table referring to her as if she had some part to play in her wedding? She perked up. In some bizarre occurrence, her stepmother's rant had been brushed aside and now the wedding was hers!

"Well, we can agree on one thing then," her father said, his eyes nervously eyeing the door. "Listen, I've got to go outside and speak to my wife, so can we make this quick?"

"No problem," her stepfather said. His voice was one of controlled authority. "Like I was saying, we know this day isn't about us. It isn't about Bernadette's stepmother either. It's about her mother."

Bernie wasn't expecting this. "What!" her father roared. "What are you saying?"

"Weddings are events for mothers to arrange. Let's face it, the fathers just aren't that important."

Her father stood up, his face the colour of a ripe plum. "First of all, there is only one father. Me. And what's this! I'm just supposed to hand over a blank check?"

"Now, now," Bernie's mother said coolly, "There is no need to raise your voice. We don't shout in our house." She paused as Bernie's father's head bounced back and forth in disbelief between each person in the room. "I have to say," she continued with no inflection, though she patted the table for emphasis, "I agree with what my husband says. Traditionally, it is the mother that…"

Bernie's father jerked backwards, his chair tipped over on to the kitchen floor. He didn't pick it up. "Come on, Bernie! We're out of here."

Like a robot, Bernie stood and followed her father out of the house. She didn't say goodbye to her mother or stepfather, not because she was offended by what just transpired; no, it was more like she had gone into anaphylactic shock.

Her father whipped open the door to his car and slammed it

shut. Bernie, wide-eyed and sputtering, climbed in too.

"Can you believe that asshole?" her father bellowed.

"Oh, I can believe it!" her stepmother answered.

What followed can only be described as a verbal assault on Bernie's mother and stepfather. Together, her father and stepmother drew strategic lines. If her mother was going to insist on paying for all the "pretty stuff," then they were going to pay for everything else.

"I'm going to make this the most lavish affair they've ever seen! I'm going to buy the most expensive food, the biggest sweet table, the best musicians. And you know what else?" he said in a rant, his driving erratic, arms flying everywhere but the steering wheel.

"What! Tell us!" her stepmother cheered him on.

"If Bernadette and Sam want the guests to drink, they'll have an open bar to choose from!" He pounded on the steering wheel, accidentally blaring the horn.

"Yes, they will!" her stepmother cried.

Hallelujah. Bernie's prayers were answered.

Wedding Truth No. 13
Eloping is not a cop out. It's an option.

When it came down to it, my real dream was not the white dress, not the garden ceremony, not the champagne toast, not collecting the expensive gifts. It was my family, seeing me off into my new life, in support of my decision and as much in love with my new husband as I was. Instead, what I had was a total mess.

Once I returned to London, my father called with a generous offer. He would pay for us to elope, no strings attached. A wedding and honeymoon in one, he called it. I wasn't the only one noticing the trouble and trauma this wedding was causing.

I didn't do it. Emotionally, I had too much invested already. I was committed to this wedding. Friends and family had already bought tickets to the States. I had my eyes on a dress. Besides, surely it couldn't get any worse?

It could. Even now, I look back on that offer and wonder how I could have been so reckless not to take it. Speaking to friends and family after, they assured me that air tickets can be transferred, plans changed. Family rifts are not so easy to mend.

Living in London was a blessing, but it was also a nightmare. After this incident, behind my back, and behind each others', my family started to arrange vendors and put down deposits. They made these arrangements, all in the name of me. When the other side discovered these acts of subterfuge, I got the blame.

I consoled myself with our one victory. We had alcohol. And we were going to need it.

Chapter Thirteen: Drug Den Wedding

Bernie was emancipated to London. In her schoolroom, surrounded by students hurling chairs at their peers, she felt calm and at peace. At home, crowded into a flat, living off cheap potato and aubergine curries for days at a time, she felt supremely satisfied.

In Detroit, where her family was better fed, living in spacious accommodation and not speaking to one another, hostility and animosity abounded.

A week earlier, on the drive to the airport, Bernie's father had asked her which, of all the places she'd seen, she'd like to marry at the most. Without pause she said, "The Detroit Manor."

He scoffed. "You liked that place? It's so old."

"It's warm. It has history." Bernie couldn't imagine a better place for her wedding. The Detroit Manor was an elegant, family home. It had no pretensions but was undoubtedly beautiful inside; from its winding banisters to its floral wallpaper and original oak flooring. A covered porch stretched along the back of the house and looked out onto lush gardens. "Dad, I could walk down that grand, wooden staircase and marry on the landing. It would be perfect."

"Perfect before or after you fall through a hole in the floor?"

"Dad!"

He reached across the seat and squeezed her knee. "I'm just kidding. Bernadette, if the Detroit Manor is what you want, then that's what we'll get you. It's very old and not that classy, but with the right flowers and decorations, I think we could make it into a great party."

High praise from the top.

First beer, and now an actual venue to drink it in. In terms of this wedding, it was extraordinary. But Bernie couldn't take a chance. "You know it's expensive though. And Mom hates it."

Not intending to, Bernie managed to say exactly what he was waiting to hear. She watched his face settle into an expression of total satisfaction. "What's she know? If I'm paying for it, let's book it!"

A week later, returning from another harrowing day at her student teaching post and still pleased she was facing unruly kids instead of her parents, Bernie received a letter through the post from her father.

Dear Bernadette,

Went by that old place you love so much, the Detroit Manor. It burned down! HA HA! Just kidding. That's a joke from your old man.

Don't worry. We booked it and it is all set. Your stepmother isn't so thrilled but she has already given the guy a list of about 100 things she wants fixed before the day. With her in charge, it will be great.

Here things are going well. The weather is freezing. Yesterday it was under zero degrees. Looking forward to seeing you in a few months. Will you be out for baseball's Opening Day? This may be the Detroit Tigers' lucky year. Don't hold your breath, though.

Love you,
Dad

Bernie thought she had better bite the bullet. She assumed her father had not told her mother anything. She'd asked him to, but he often conveniently forgot if it meant speaking to her mother.

Holding the phone, Bernie paced up and down in her cramped sitting room. Her flatmates wouldn't be home for hours. This was the perfect time. She brought the phone up to dial. She dropped her arm. She raised it again. The phone shouted at her. It had a will of its own! Bernie threw it on the settee where it continued to ring and ring. Reluctantly, she plucked the animal from its cushion.

"Hello?" she said hesitantly.

"Bernadette!" Her mother sounded ready for battle, self-assured and dynamic.

"Hi Mom," Bernie said. She smacked her head with her hand. How did her mother know? She always knew when something was up. She had a mother's insight, verging on wizardry.

"So when I was I going to find out about this, Bernadette? When I received my invitation? When my guests RSVP'd? Tell me." Her mother's voice was measured, controlled.

"I thought you would find out when Dad called you to discuss it. I'm assuming he didn't?"

"Of course he did not. Nor did you share this information with me. Do you know how I found out, Bernadette?" This was a rhetorical question. Not a trap Bernie was likely to fall into. She stayed silent. "You know how? The Detroit Manor just called me. On the phone. They wanted to know when I wanted to come down for a tasting of their menu." In the background, Bernie heard cupboard doors open and slam shut, dishes clattering into the dishwasher, the refrigerator door cracking into a wall as it repelled from a harsh kick. Her mother's voice sounded measured but her anger was not. "I told them they must be mistaken. I made no deposit at the Detroit Manor. I would never allow my daughter to marry there."

"You told them that?" Bernie was worried now. Did she cancel the venue? Could she do that if she hadn't put down the deposit?

"I did indeed. But the bride's mother isn't important enough to decide where her daughter will get married. A deposit has been paid." Bernie ached with relief. Until that moment, she had no idea how entrenched the place had become in her wedding fantasy. "Now Bernadette. I have a very clear idea of what my daughter's perfect wedding day will be like and the Detroit Manor does not fit in with my vision for you."

Bernie paused. This was an argument she'd heard before. "Mom," she said carefully, "what about the perfect wedding I envision for myself?"

Her mother's exasperation pelted Bernie through the phone, but she didn't raise her voice. "I won't settle for anything less than perfect for my little girl."

"Meaning you want me to cancel the Detroit Manor." Bernie began designing speeches of resignation in her mind to deliver to her father.

"Meaning you may want to get married there, and I will support your decision, but I will not support you financially. And of course," Bernie's mother said as almost an afterthought, "you will be forcing me to turn my guests away."

Her mother was prone to drastic threats, but this was unusually harsh. "What? Turn your guests away? I want your guests to come."

"But when you put my friends and family in danger by holding your wedding in such a bad area, you leave me no choice. That part of Detroit is run-down, full of drug addicts and prostitutes. I won't have my guests assaulted. So you see, it is out of my control. You have done this, Bernadette."

This was a fundamental moment, not only in the wedding, but also in Bernie's relationship with her mother. If Bernie relented, she gave in to her mother's irrational demands, as well as scored her a victory point in the Parental War. On the other hand, her mother's stubborn nature meant that this was no idle threat. Take a stand and her mother might not invite a single person.

"Mom, your real issue is not the place. The Detroit Manor is fine. The problem is you feel the decision has been taken out of your hands. If Dad had called you to discuss it, we probably wouldn't be having this conversation right now."

Her mother huffed on the other end. "Bernadette, it is your decision. If you don't want our side to attend the wedding, then you are welcome to stick with the Detroit Mansion."

Earlier in the conversation, Bernie had felt the familiar solid ground of rationality falling away beneath her as she began to crumble in the face of another of her mother's demands. But Bernie was sick of crumbling. She was sick of her wedding becoming another means by which her devotion could be proved to one parent or another. She felt her resolve build and tried again. "Mom, let me make this perfectly clear. I want you at the wedding. I want your guests at the wedding. The Detroit Manor is not in a bad part of town. You are angry, and maybe you have a right to be, but it is your choice if you decide not to invite anyone. You wanted to pay for all the pretty things. You opted out of the rest."

Bernie caught a glance of herself in the mirror. She shadow-boxed at her reflection. On the other end of the line was total silence. "Down for the count," Bernie thought smugly to herself.

Bernadette's mother always rose to a challenge. Just before she hung up on her daughter, she made one final critique of the situation. "Fine, Bernadette. You make the biggest mistake of your life. Don't say I didn't warn you."

*   *   *

Bernadette phoned her father. What could she do? She would have to give in. Her mother had won again.

She explained the situation to her father. She expected him to grumble and give in, like she was about to do. Instead, he must have seen this as a fundamental moment as well. "Who cares?" he said triumphantly.

"Dad," Bernie pleaded, "she isn't going to bring a single guest."

"Like they'll be missed. All two of them."

Bernie rolled her eyes. "That's great, Dad. Very mature."

"You want maturity, speak to your mother. You want common sense, see me."

Wedding Truth No. 14

There's a reason why Julia Roberts jumped ship so frequently in 'The Runaway Bride'. And it wasn't Richard Gere.

Hold to your guns, Bride! Keep strong! Fight the power! Good luck to you, because you are going to need it.

The only people who laugh at the idea that planning a wedding is an act of torture are those people who are blessedly single. Brides know different. For every bride that has no problem with her own family, it's her fiance's she has to deal with, or her growing overdraft, or her waistline, or her jealous best friend, or any number of hurdles.

My family made my wedding a war. My venue, the battlefield. My wishes, casualties. I felt like I was drowning. I was supposed to turn to my parents for advice in these situations. When your parents are the problem, there isn't anyone to turn to. It is an incredible feeling of isolation.

I heard a priest once say that his main job was to see his congregation through the milestones of life: birth, marriage, death; christening, wedding, funeral. This event is one of the most momentous of a woman's life. It should feel good, but with that kind of significance and pressure, it's no wonder that it doesn't.

Chapter Fourteen: Reception in Ruins

Bernie spent two months of grindingly painful anticipation waiting for her mother to call her in London. Her mother had incredible resilience. She could wait out anything.

Her father relished the silence.

"Bernie," he said one night over the phone, "two months from yesterday, guess where we were?"

He loved this game. Bernie racked her brain. "I was at home in Detroit – "

"Yeah – " He giggled.

"The Pancake House? Devouring a Big German Pancake?"

"Ha! I wish!" He laughed. "No, we were at your mother's. She was insulting my wife and you were sulking as usual."

Bernie's stomach turned with the memory. "What do you mean 'as usual'? From what I remember, I wasn't even a part of the proceedings."

He laughed louder. "Now, ask me why I am in such a good mood."

Even Bernie smiled now. It was infectious, even if inane. "Okay, why?"

"Because it's been two months since that day and that's two months since I last saw your mother." He roared with great satisfaction.

"Very funny, Dad," Bernie said flatly. "Maybe it's been two lovely months for you, but they haven't been the greatest for me.

She still isn't speaking to me."

"No? Think of it as a blessing."

"Dad!"

"Tell you what," he said. "I will make the first move. I've had a two-month vacation. Time to get back to work!"

Bernie cheered instantly. "Really? You mean it?"

"No, but you have fun." He roared again.

Bernie groaned. "Thanks, Dad."

"Yep. No prob."

*   *   *

Bernie bit the bullet. She called her mother. She expected screaming down the phone or curt small talk, but in typical form, her mother responded bizarrely. She pretended as if nothing had happened.

"Oh, honey! It's so nice to hear from you." Her voice exuded the kind of sugary warmth reserved for the scripts of Hollywood family films. Bernie panicked immediately.

"And it is nice to talk to you," Bernie said, trialling a complimentary tone. "We haven't spoken," she stopped to swallow her dignity, "for awhile and I thought maybe we should catch up."

"About?" The pick-and-choose amnesia had struck again. Her mother was the expert on diversionary practices.

"The wedding?"

"Oh, that." The implication was that the wedding was far, far from important to her. "It's a good thing you called, actually. I have some terrible news for you."

"Oh, God. What's happened?" Bernie's voice pitched violently. "What's wrong? Is something wrong?"

"Well, it won't affect my guests much since you won't let them share in your day – " Her mother dangled this comment smugly before continuing, but Bernie ignored it. "But you should know that the Detroit Manor is up for sale."

"For sale!"

"Admittedly, I was never very happy with the Detroit Manor,

but nonetheless I drove by it the other day, just to check on it for you and I saw the sign. I am very concerned. Now don't take this the wrong way, but I also noticed the porch was flooded and the front window smashed."

"Flooded? Smashed?" Bernie sounded like a scratched record.

Her mother murmured with pleasure, "Bernadette, I know you don't want to hear this, but you have a big, very adult decision to make. Just remember, my offer to help out still stands if you need to get out of this situation. I value you and your choices."

Bernadette hung up, shell-shocked. Was her mother right? Was the Detroit Manor really falling apart? Was it being sold up, out from under her feet? Deposits had been paid! Surely they couldn't sell when her father has already put down a deposit!

But in her heart Bernie knew they could. Yet another reminder that this wedding was not the event of the century, as it felt like to her. Actually, in the grand scheme of things, a wedding mattered very little.

She called Anne. Her voice shook with nerves and wedding torment. "I need you to do a drive-by."

"You want me to take someone out? Like with a gun? That's very Detroit." Anne sounded amused.

Bernie was not. "No, I need you to drive by the Detroit Manor. My mother claims it's a flooded wreck and about to be sold. I need to know: is she telling the truth or exaggerating to infuriate me?"

Anne hummed. "Well I can answer that for you right now. She is exaggerating. She is trying to infuriate you. She's probably also telling the truth."

"What! Oh, God." Bernie started pacing the lounge furiously. "So it is true. You've been there! The place is falling down and all my guests will need rain gear." She groaned. "No! It's worse. Oh, tell me it hasn't been sold!"

Anne giggled. "Wow. This wedding really is driving you insane, isn't it?"

Bernie could not hide the manic tone in her voice. "Yes! Yes, it is!"

"Okay, worry-wart, calm down." Anne stopped giggling and

tried to instil a measure of sanity into the conversation. "I was just joking around. I haven't been there. I'm just working off what I know of your mother, mainly that she likes to win, and, unfortunately, at least for you right now, she is no liar."

Bernie plopped into a chair. "Please, Anne. Please check it out for me. I'm over here and I can't do it myself." She took a deep breath and then admitted solemnly, though she felt ridiculous, "I feel like I'm losing my mind here."

Anne put on an air of professionalism. "I'm on the case. Leave it to me."

*　　*　　*

The next day Anne called in her report. "Do you want the good news or the bad news?" she said.

Bernie took a deep breath. Just the fact that there was bad news made her heart go into palpitations. "The good news."

"The Detroit Manor isn't for sale. Though the house next door is."

Bernie's voice chirped back at Anne in a repetition of total lunacy. "Okay, okay. The house isn't for sale, not for sale. The reception venue is still available. Available and not for sale." She paced back and forth, balancing her feet on the edge of the rug in the lounge like a tightrope.

"Bernie, maybe I should call you back. You sound like you are ready for a total mental collapse."

"BAD NEWS NOW." Bernie wasn't about to wait for later.

"Okay, fine. Your call. The thing is, your mother wasn't exaggerating. The house looks nothing like what it did back when we saw it. The front window is smashed. It's covered over in clingfilm at the moment. No one's bothered to sweep up the broken glass, which is now imbedded in the lawn. It rained two nights back and the porch is indeed flooded, even after all that time. The backyard looks like a boggy marsh and the dirt drive isn't looking all that pretty either, think swampland, and you'd be close." Anne waited for a response. She continued to wait. And wait. "Bernie?"

"That's it then," a small voice squeaked from the other line.

"It seems so," Anne admitted.

"You know the worst of it?"

Anne rushed in to stop her. "Don't worry. We'll find you another place. There are bound to be tons of places free. We have five months to find one."

"No, that's not it. There is something more terrible."

"Yes?"

Bernie swallowed. "She's won."

*   *   *

Bernie called her father immediately to renegotiate. He was far from pleased. "The place is perfectly good, Bernadette," he said. "Rather than lose my deposit, we just call up the guy. He'll fix the window."

Bernie countered insistently, "And the glass? And the porch? And my mother?"

"Well, nobody can fix her, but we can try for the rest," he grumbled.

Bernie was not amused. She tried a new angle. "Dad, you may lose your deposit, but Mom won't give any money to the Detroit Manor. This way she pays, so you save money. Plus, she'll actually invite people and we won't have to listen to her complaints."

"Reality check, Bernie. Your mom will pick a new place, not us. It will be twice as expensive as the last one. She'll say she'll help pay, but won't. To top it off, this time, instead of just my guests, I'll be paying for hers too."

There was some truth in this. Actually, Bernie already knew where the new place was and how much it cost. How did she know? A crisp, thick envelope from her mother had arrived yesterday full of colour photos and brochure materials advertising Pine Mansion. Bernie and her mother had visited it the previous summer and her mother had not stopped raving about it since. And her father was right. Pine Mansion was expensive.

Along with the carefully compiled information pack, Bernie's mother enclosed a note:

Dear Bernadette,

I know we said that we'd talk about it further, but I could not resist! I've enclosed information on Pine Mansion. I know you will love it there. When I visited the other day, I just felt it was perfect for my daughter. The location in the hills, the mansion itself (much bigger than I recalled), the gardens. Oh, you should see it! I've already pencilled us in a date!

Now, I don't want you to worry yourself over the cost. Your father has plenty of money to pay for it. But just so it is fair, I will pay towards it as well. I always keep my end of a bargain!

Besides, that Detroit Manor was so terrible. I know you will agree with me there! This way, you will have the wonderful day I've always dreamed you would. And you know what I always say Bernadette:

When life gives you lemons, make lemonade!

Love you,

Mom

P.S. Guess what I found out when I pencilled us in at Pine Mansion? The wedding planner is Marnie, the same woman who planned your Sweet Sixteen party. How much fun was that? Remember the hayride, the dancing, the food? Everything is falling into place! Hurrah!

Wedding Truth No. 15

There is no place for pride in wedding planning. Grovelling can get you everywhere.

Yes, I remembered my Sweet Sixteen. We ate hotdogs. You can do that for a teenager. The thought that the same woman would cater my wedding, along with arranging all the other details on the day, didn't instil the confidence in me that it did in my mother.

With my reception hall swimming and smashed, and even my father witnessing it for himself, I could resist no more. I weighed up my options. I could get married in a ruined old house with no guests on my mother's side, or I could relent and try someplace else that we could all agree on. My father would lose his deposit and all I'd lose was a bit of pride.

With only five months before the wedding, I frantically appealed to my father's good will. Even he admitted Pine Mansion had something for everyone. For my mother, it wasn't in Detroit. The Mansion rested up in the green hills outside the city. For my father, it wasn't old and for my stepmother, it was attached to a golf course. And finally, for me, I had my high ceilings, lush gardens, wood panelled rooms and elegant stained-glass windows. More importantly, the gazebo outside, the heart of our ceremony, rested at the edge of a cliff looking out over the highest vantage point in south-east Michigan. From that height and angle, the golf course below disappeared against the panorama of the rolling countryside.

It might have just been perfect.

Chapter Fifteen: Pecking Order... The Invites

Hindsight is the bane of many a heroine's life. In a horror movie, there is the joy and terror of watching helplessly as a pneumatic, blonde teenager sneaks upstairs to meet her boyfriend for a quick shag while a mask wearing, chainsaw wielding, asylum escapee lies in wait behind her dresser.

Who called out to Bernie? When she and Sam decided to save their money for months and surprise her parents by offering to pay for the invitations, who shouted out a warning? The world was eerily quiet.

It was to be a horror film of their own making, and just as chilling. Sam and Bernie, innocent, ignorant, linked hands and smiled into one another's eyes, as they climbed the stairs to a grisly end.

They had only wanted to help out, to contribute and not feel like such scroungers. Bernie imagined her parents would welcome the opportunity to shed some of their burden. She thought they would appreciate her contribution.

What do Bernie and Sam not know, that everyone else who has ever planned a wedding, do? Invitations are second only to seating plans in ridiculous complexity:

1. Invitations represent the wedding. Elements of snobbery, parents call this etiquette, abound here. The script, the weight of the paper, the texture of the paper, the lining of the envelope, all speak volumes about what kind of people your people are, even if your people are not those kind of people. Confused? Read on.

2. The order of the names denotes who the most important member of the family is.

3. The order of the names denotes who paid the most and who is cheap.

4. If the bride and groom aren't paying, they aren't listed so much as inserted.

When Bernie called her parents to share how, despite their precarious financial state, she and Sam would lift this one small but fundamental burden of the wedding, her parents were horrified. Their responses mimicked the other's exactly. "Don't order them until you mail us the proofs."

It is at this moment that the audience starts to shout, "He's got a knife! Run!"

Instead, Bernie kept climbing those stairs. The following week, the demolition of the rainforests began. Day after day, bulging envelopes brimming with sample invitations began arriving. She pored over every flower and lace, little pink bird and confetti. Her fingers stroked the variety of textured white, off-white, antique cream and eggshell stationery.

Meanwhile, her parents started sending her their own samples. They called her in hourly shifts expressing their gratitude but willingness to relieve her of her invitation duties. They offered to pay double, triple, towards stationary from the most expensive and exclusive ranges available. They appealed to her sense of duty to her finances. They painted nightmarish visions of the costs and her future mounting debts. They offered to allow her to invest her money in tablecloths, party favours, napkin holders. Most importantly, they understood why she might want to backtrack on her offer and, not to worry, they were okay with that.

Bernie acted the dutiful daughter. She stood her ground, but conceded that proofs should be sent to each parental home. Incidentally, though both parents were very concerned about their placement in relation to one another and the inclusion of their partners (which both sides made clear the other would leave out on purpose), they seemed entirely fine with how Sam's parents were listed, which of course they all assumed was last.

121

Finally, Bernie negotiated with her mother to allow her father to be listed first on the invites. This was no small task. She appealed to her mother's sense of style, etiquette and responsibility.

"Not only are they elegant, Mother, but they list the venue you chose in the end, the one you discovered. Not only did Dad not fight us on the change," and here she swallowed her pride, "to a more suitable location, but he gave up his deposit."

Bernie listened respectfully to the silence of her mother calculating the personal loss of territory if she relinquished her place on the invites.

"Bernadette," she began finally, "as you are aware, mothers traditionally are listed first. I just want what is appropriate. But I suppose I'll have to be the more gracious party. Obviously I will expect to see the proofs anyway."

Bernadette's irritation at this lack of trust flared up, but she agreed. "I'll send you a copy," she said.

Once she sent off her parents' proofs, Bernie thought that would be the end of it. But when her father's proof was returned to her, she noticed one small change made.

Listed first amongst all the names on the invites was her stepmother. Bernie gasped at this roadblock. Nothing had been mentioned to her of this fundamental change in seniority. Bernie's mother would have a conniption. Conveniently, her father and stepmother left for a two-week cruise holiday after they sent their changes. They couldn't be reached. The invitations had to be ordered. Weddings wait for no man, not even when that man's the dad.

"You are in a world of shit," Beth said when Bernie asked her about it. "Imagine a large outhouse with you resting at the bottom. Your whole world, shit."

Bernie rolled her eyes. Beth was prone to exaggeration. "It isn't that bad."

Beth cackled across the phone at her in a way only a sister who's been there can. "Oh, Bernadette. I pity you."

"Beth, I'm only trying to be reasonable. I'm trying to make an informed choice. Dad's gone. Advise me. They have to be ordered."

"Whatever you do, someone's gonna kill you. My advice is to stay out of the country for as long as you can."

"But why, I don't understand."

Beth sighed in exasperation. "They're our parents, Bernadette. If there is no reason, they'll find one."

A terrible dilemma imposed itself upon Bernie. Would she wait it out, allowing her stepmother to return and engage her in the inevitable lecture on the necessity of her being placed first? Or would Bernie go forth, listing her father first, as he conceived her, thereby forgoing the inevitable lecture from her mother on the vile disrespect of a daughter who would dare list her stepmother before her own father and mother?

At this point in the game, the only inevitability was a lecture. As Bernie and Sam finally controlled one aspect of the wedding, she took a brave leap. She placed the order.

A gorgeous thrill of risk and adventure surged through Bernie as she phoned the purchasing number! Then, two weeks later, Bernie delighted over her sense of accomplishment when she cracked open the white, imprinted box and gazed upon her invitations for the first time. Proudly, she presented them to her flatmates to cheers and, she was certain, notes of awe in their voices. Pride cometh before the fall.

As her parents could not agree on who should address the invitations (her mother wrote in beautiful calligraphy, but her father and stepmother insisted that her mother would purposely send them to the wrong people if she was given the honour of addressing them), Bernie sent each set of parents their own box of invitations. With great care, she carefully wrapped them in layers of newspaper and packed them securely in boxes. Each set was completed with return envelopes, printed in advance with each parents' address, ensuring the response arrived in the hands of the side the guest was attached to. God forbid any guest should think the other parent had more control over the RSVPs!

The next week, after receiving his package of invitations, Bernie's father called her. His voice was dour and grim. "Bernie," he said, "we received your invitations today and were shocked to discover you made changes without consulting us."

Bernie explained how he'd been out of town, weddings waiting for no man, etc. Her father didn't buy it. "Bernie, because you have ignored our wishes, we have no choice but to not use these invitations. We can't send these out to our friends."

Bernie had not expected this. A lecture, yes; total dismissal, no. She tried nonetheless to convince him. "Dad, the invitations are beautiful. You are listed first. You are my dad! You conceived me! You are both still ahead of my mother, who has relinquished her moment in the sun to be listed on the second line."

"That may be true, but regardless, we are very disappointed in you. You went behind our backs. You went against our wishes."

Bernie started to cry. No one on her father's side would see the one thing she actually purchased. "Do you hate them? Are they ugly? Is it so terrible that a daughter would want her father's name to come first? I'm proud you are my dad."

He sighed when he heard her crying and his tone lightened from admonishing to troubled. "Bernadette, we've gone around and asked all the best stationery stores in town. It is not proper etiquette to list the man's name first. "

Bernie angered. "You mean she has. She has gone around and bullied people into saying that. Does she always have to be number one? Does she always have to get exactly what she wants?"

Her father's voice rose again. "Bernie, don't talk about my wife using that tone. Without her, there would be no wedding at all." He paused and tried again. "We are getting our own invitations and that is final."

Bernie started weeping. Sam burst into the room, concerned. "I've got to go," she mumbled to her father and hung up the phone.

At this point, Bernie thought nothing else could go wrong. How could it? Her mother had already threatened to uninvite all her guests, but that situation had been averted. Now, her father had dealt her a terrible blow. The chains that bound her to this wedding meant she could only accept the decision he made.

"Everything about this wedding may be chosen by someone

else," Sam said stroking her hair that night, "but not us Bernie. We chose each other. And if we can get through this, we can make it through much of what life is going to throw at us."

While Sam said these sensible things to her, he was seething. From that night on, if he answered the phone to find one of Bernie's parents on the other end, he told them she was out. Out of respect for Bernie, he said nothing else. He couldn't disrespect them, but he could protect Bernie from hearing more of their nonsense.

Sam's reach only stretched so far. The following week, with one letter, Bernie's mother destroyed all her hopes. It came through the letterbox marked "Priority Mail":

Dear Bernie,

Your invitations, which arrived today, caused me terrible pain.

First of all, I am insulted by the delivery and presentation of them. They have been carelessly thrown together along with some old newspapers of yours and are, as they are, undeliverable.

I had informed you that raised print was necessary for a proper, formal wedding invitation only to discover that, against my wishes, you have purchased plain invitations as one could print from any photocopier. Furthermore, the print and typeface are common and totally unsuitable for a grand event.

The impression you give your guests, my guests as well, remember, should be one of elegance and romance. Instead you have flung these cheap invitations at me with no regard to my feelings.

Since you began planning this wedding, you have turned your back on all my help and ideas. Rather than consult with me, you gave your wedding over to your father's wife. You ignored my advice and avoided exploring options with me. I can only imagine this is because you are not interested in my ideas. You minimise what I have to say, yet, are interested in me helping fund your wedding.

Furthermore, though your father and his wife insulted me from day one, you never stuck up for me or attempted to stop them. I don't understand how a caring daughter could do this to her mother, especially one who has sacrificed so much and asked for so little in return. I gave you life, Bernadette.

The kind of daughter who does this is not the kind I can call my own. These are appalling things I never would have raised you to do, and done with the kind of contempt I do not deserve. You have never apologised for the serious wrongs you have brought upon our family. You leave me no option. No longer can I consider myself your mother, or you my daughter. I wish you the best in life, future success and happiness in your marriage but I can not participate in that wedding or your life any longer. This is a consequence of your decisions. You have betrayed our trust and violated the bond we share.

Goodbye, Bernadette.

Wedding Truth No. 16

There are more important things than your wedding.

If I had known that getting married would end my relationship with my mother, I would not have done it. Eloping is the best option sometimes.

No party is worth losing your mother over. For days after I received her letter, I cried. I woke up in tears and spent the day sobbing. I felt like I had lost her, forever. I mourned our relationship. I mourned a woman I would never again speak to, laugh with, share cherished moments with.

I arrived the following day at my teaching post and sobbed as soon as my advisor spoke to me. He sent me home and I never finished that final placement. Luckily, they passed me anyway.

Struggling to cope, my mind always returned to the devastating concept that she had made a deliberate choice to spend her life without me in it. When she received those invitations, she took the lack of raised print as a personal affront, the final one. Weighing the options, she decided it better to cut me out of her life. She'd justified it to me in a letter.

For my father and stepmother, it was a turning point. Horrified and racked with guilt, my father called me daily. My stepmother called me personally to apologise. "You decide," she said with great sympathy. "If you can't do the wedding now, we'll all understand." I remember very well the kindness my stepmother showed me then. After all her work, she was genuinely willing to forget the whole event.

I took solace in this. But nothing, no apology from my father and stepmother, no gentle understanding of my feelings, could replace my mother. Where was she?

Chapter Sixteen: Mom on the Run

Bernie never wanted to stumble on her mother's words again. But days later, the letter continued to haunt her from its home, in the bottom drawer of her dresser, concealed by pyjamas, socks and tights. Without reading it again, Bernie exhumed it from under the clothes and folded it back into thirds. On the top page, above her mother's beautiful calligraphy, Bernie wrote simply, "You can't possibly mean all this so I am returning it to you." Gingerly, she placed it into a fresh envelope, wrote her mother's address on the front, folded down the flap, pressed the adhesive closed and cried.

She cried for ever wanting to get married. She cried for imagining that she deserved a wedding in which her parents would be proud. She cried for putting Sam through such a trauma. She cried for the embarrassment and humiliation this would bring. She cried for the loss of her mother. She cried and cried and cried.

Weeks passed without word from her mother. Not that she expected to hear from her. Even though her mother's letter had been returned, Bernie knew she would not call to apologize or to take it all back. Bernie expected nothing, and that's what she received. No word. No letter. No email. No phone call.

Bernie watched her world fog over. She stumbled through daily routines and avoided as much of life as she could. She spent long hours soaking in baths and devoting herself to her teaching dissertation. Anything to while away the days and forget.

Sam watched helplessly as Bernie limped through the next

month. What he wanted to do was reach across the Atlantic Ocean and strangle Bernie's mother. Without any hope of that happening, he held Bernie and comforted her as best he could.

One day, home alone working on her dissertation, the phone rang. Bernie picked it up, her voice limp and indifferent.

"Bernadette, this is your mother."

Bernie didn't say anything. She couldn't make her tongue work. It lay flat and heavy with emotion in her mouth. Her eyes welled with tears and they streamed down her face silently. Her mother sounded so normal. Why was she calling her? Was her mother about to confirm all she said in her letter? Was it to rub in one final criticism?

"Bernie? Bernadette, are you there?"

Bernie moaned an acknowledgement, but kept her thoughts silent.

"Bernadette. I sent you my letter weeks ago and you haven't responded." Her mother sounded hurt, as if Bernie had paid her the terrible offence instead of the other way around.

"I did respond. I sent it back."

"I meant a meaningful response."

Bernie's eyes continued to fill with tears, but her voice was remarkably calm. "Mother, why are you calling me? You told me our relationship was over. You disowned me."

"You abandoned me, Bernadette," her mother responded indignantly. "You did this, not me. I'm only waiting for an apology."

"I don't understand…" Bernie stammered.

"An apology. And of course," her mother added, "you need to consider my feelings more. My ideas."

Bernie sat stunned. Her mother waited on the other line expecting an apology. She waited for Bernie to beg forgiveness. Bernie's resilience and anger grew. "Was this all some kind of scare tactic to get your say in my wedding? Were you joking? Because I took you seriously."

"I was serious. Very much. I expect you to listen to me and make some relevant changes."

Bernie's voice crackled with anger. "I can't take back wanting to marry Sam. I can't take back wanting both my parents involved in my life. I'm not going to apologise for all of you trying to hurt each other through me. And I'm not going to apologise for you disowning me as a result." Her voice deepened. "You made your decision and it was a terrible one."

Her mother's voice sounded weaker. Was she crying? "You made me do it, Bernadette. You have been so awful to me. I had no choice."

Bernadette screamed into the phone. "Shut up! I can't take this anymore. This has destroyed me! What are you doing? Why are you cutting me out of your life for the sake of control of the wedding? What can be so important about this that is more important than your relationship with me?" Bernadette petered off, sobbing uncontrollably.

Her mother's voice was firm on the other end. "You are the one who risked our relationship over this wedding. You gambled it away to please your father's wife."

"No." Bernadette resolved not to give in to this onslaught. "You have done this. I didn't ask you to turn your back on me."

"Bernadette, do you mean to say you have nothing to apologise for?"

"No, I am sorry. I'm sorry I started this whole thing to begin with. I'm sorry I thought my parents were mature enough to put their ill feelings behind them. I'm sorry I have to go to Wales this weekend and explain to Sam's parents that my mother won't be at my wedding and hope they don't hold it against me."

Silence deadened the line. Bernie sobbed and blew her nose. She looked at the clock. When would Sam be home? When would this all be over?

Her mother finally broke the silence. "You are going to Wales this weekend?"

Still sniffling, Bernie replied. "Yes, it will be embarrassing and painful, but I will do it because at least one of us is mature enough to face problems head on. Someone's got to tell them."

"Oh." Maybe her mother hadn't considered this. People would

have to know that she wasn't coming. Maybe she expected Bernie to give in to her demands. Because Bernie didn't, her mother would have to follow through with her threats. She wouldn't attend the wedding. "Well, if that's the way you want it. Then goodbye." She hung up the phone and Bernie was left staring at the receiver, her relationship with her mother in ruins.

* * *

For hours on the train to Wales, Bernie rehearsed her speech to her future in-laws. Sam held her hand as she stared out the window at the rolling English hills, then at the inevitable downpour as they crossed the Severn Bridge into Wales. Rain pelted against the train, mimicking Bernie's own tears.

Arriving at Sam's home, his mum greeted them with welcoming hugs. Before they hit the sitting room though, Bernie already felt overwhelmed. The magnitude of admitting such a grand personal failure pressed her.

"I need to speak with you," she said with urgency.

"Not a problem," Sam's mum responded. "Have a cup of tea first. Settle down and then we'll talk."

"But it's really important. It's about the wedding."

"Honestly, Mum, I think you need to hear this," Sam said.

"It's nothing that can't wait a few moments. Why don't you go down to the kitchen and I'll help Sam bring your things upstairs." Bernie stood motionless. "Now, now," Sam's mum continued, "you go on into the kitchen now."

Bernie sighed, but followed her instructions. She still wasn't sure how she would tell them anyway. What would they think of her when they found out her own mother hated her so much?

Carefully, she walked through the long, narrow corridors of their terraced house, running her hands along the cool walls, opening and shutting each door leading to the kitchen.

Bernie had just turned on the kettle as Sam's father bowled into the room. He was loud and red-faced as usual, but this time, Bernie took it as a sign.

"We received a call from your mother today," he said gravely setting his purchases on the table.

Bernie replied, without thinking, "Oh, shit." She'd been right; he was red-faced for a reason. He agreed with her mother. He hated her. They all hated her. Her mother had beaten her to it.

Feelings of desperation swelled in her. Bernie couldn't imagine how these nice people, who barely knew her, would be able to ignore the calm, destructive force of her mother. What kind of horrible person had her mother made her out to be? The kind that thinks a wedding is more important than her family? The kind that brushes asides years of maternal dedication? The kind of selfish, heartless child they wouldn't want in their own family?

"Don't worry," he said, eyes twinkling. "We told her we loved you and it didn't matter to us. We heard her out, but you're our family too now, Bernie. Besides, I imagine this thing with your mother will work itself out."

"You do?" Bernie radiated shock and relief.

"Yes. Why shouldn't it? It's only a wedding after all. Of course, we did tell her we hoped that she'd change her mind. And don't worry girl, I'm sure she will." A big laugh burst from his chest. "You know, the same thing happened to us when we got married?"

"Really? Your mother disowned you?"

"No, but hers did. Well, sort of. I asked for her hand, but they wouldn't give it to me. They made me wait a whole year to prove myself and then when it came to planning the wedding, her mother refused to come. Not my biggest fans, see."

"And what happened?" Bernie asked.

"Oh, they came in the end. But not before a lot of tears were shed. I'm sure the same thing will happen for you." Another big barrel laugh erupted from him. "And if she doesn't," he continued with a wink, "we'll send the Welsh Taffia after her. Very frightening. Almost like the real mafia."

Bernie noticed she was breathing again. She remembered the kettle and not knowing what to say to express her extreme gratitude for this moment, she did something very British. "Can I make you a cup of tea?" she asked.

"Lovely," he said. Then he reached behind him and pulled from his shopping bag a gold tea tray emblazoned with the Welsh flag and a brown coffee mug in the shape of rugby hero Gareth Edward's head. "What do you think, girl? This," he indicated the rugby player's head, "20p! And this," he lifted the gold tray, "70p! Can you believe it? Those charity shops, what a find!"

Bernie handed him his cup of tea and smiled appreciatively. "You're absolutely right. Quite a find."

Wedding Truth No. 17

Much as you would like them to, weddings change nothing.

Some people think that a wedding will be the answer to their happiness. It certainly occupies your life for a while, makes you feel important for a day, allows you to be lavished with gifts like never before, even look the most amazing you ever will. But these are false and fleeting virtues.

If you are getting married for these reasons, you are marrying for the wrong reasons. Your friends won't tell you this, so I will. Marriage will not solve the relationship issues with your boyfriend. If you tell yourself, once we're married he will be different, you are wrong. Furthermore, your family will not start respecting you more and caring for you differently and neither will his.

Weddings are meant to make brides feel transformed like Cinderella. But once the night is over, much like Cinderella, you will return to the doldrums of normal life. Post-wedding, everything will be the same.

You are just like me. A Cinderella-in-waiting. Just like me, you will have to face the same problems and difficulties before as after. At this point in my wedding, I was facing, not only these problems but also this realisation. No one was going to wave a magic wand over my family or my life. I'd have to face my problems, just like you.

On the other hand, you may find, as I did, the most unexpected of allies. My husband's parents were those people for me. If I can pinpoint one fairy godmother moment in this whole fiasco, it was that conversation in a little kitchen in Wales.

Chapter Seventeen: A Rabbi walks into a bar...

Bernie couldn't marry the discontent of her mother with the absolute conviction that she should spend her life with Sam. The more she thought about it, the more out of control she felt.

"You need to put this behind you," Sam told her.

"How?" Bernie's sullen depression made her feel the impossibility of any resolution.

Sam said, "You could move on, focus on something good. There is still our marriage to consider. Don't we deserve a celebration?"

To Bernie the gulf between her actual feelings and the idea of celebrating stretched further than the Atlantic Ocean. Her marriage, the important part, the rest of her life with Sam, lay even further. She thought of nothing else but jumping through the hurdles of the wedding. Rationally, she knew it would pass, but in the here and now, it felt like her whole world. Thoughts of a future minus wedding plans, a future where her life alongside her husband began, seemed like a total fantasy. In all the hassle of the wedding, she'd put aside her and Sam's future. Her life needed a kick-start and she needed a kick in the ass.

That night her stepmother phoned. Sam answered. In the past few weeks, he'd gotten into the habit of screening Bernie's calls. He poked his head out through the kitchen door to make sure Bernie wasn't around and spoke quietly into the phone.

"Hello?"

"Oh Sam! How is our little Boo-Boo?"

"Your um, Boo-Boo is fine," he said assuming she meant Bernie.

"Really, Sam honey. Give it to me straight. Her father is killing himself over here worrying."

Sam cleared his throat. "Well if you really want to know, she's devastated. She's walking around like a zombie. She – "

"Oy gevalt. She sounds terrible. What kind of mother does this to a daughter?"

"I suppose she – "

"A terrible one, I'll tell you. That woman doesn't know what she is missing in our Bernadette. You know what I mean?"

"Yes, I –"

"I wish I could do something. You know?"

Sam paused. If he started speaking again, he feared he wouldn't get anything more than two words in. "May I say something?"

"Yes! Of course! Anything."

He pulled his thoughts together. "I'm really worried about Bernie."

"We all are."

His voice deepened. "Really worried."

He caught her attention. "Tell me more," she said solemnly.

"This fight over the wedding has cost Bernie her relationship with her mother. Her mother blames Bernie for the trouble between you lot."

"But we didn't start this," her voice clipped.

His voice rose noticeably, uncontrollably. "And Bernie did? You all acted like children and now Bernie is paying the price."

"Now wait a minute," her voice grew shrill. "We've been very supportive of Bernie."

"Supportive! Is putting Bernie in the middle of this mess, making her your go between supportive?"

"Sam, you need to calm down. I don't deserve to be yelled at. What right do you have to speak to me this way?"

Sam took a deep breath before he spoke again. Anger boiled inside him, but he gathered his emotions. "Bernie is an absolute mess. She needs your help. She needs her father to do something, besides just apologise to her. He needs to contact her mother."

"Contact her! You must be kidding. Even if he does, she's not going to speak to him."

"He is the link that binds them at the moment. He is the reason she is not speaking to Bernie and he is her father. Maybe he can't fix anything, but at least Bernie will know he tried. And maybe then she'll have some hope of speaking to her mother again, someday."

Bernie's stepmother sounded exasperated now, but no longer shouted back at him. "It doesn't matter how angry you get Sam. She'll never speak to him."

"I'm only looking out for Bernie. This is what she needs. Can you ask him to speak to her? For Bernie's sake?"

"Okay," she said. "Fine. We aren't turning our backs on her like her mother did." Sam's outburst angered her, but she resolved to do as he asked. "I'll speak to her father," she said, "I'll do it."

Sam felt relief. He knew Bernie's stepmother would hold to her promise. Maybe it wouldn't solve anything, but at least Bernie would see that one side of the family was finally rooting for her.

On the other hand, he felt relief for another reason. For weeks he held back from calling Bernie's parents and raining down a verbal hell upon them. Now he had confirmation that, since actually wringing their necks was out of the question, at least he'd be able to hold his own against them. If Bernie couldn't defend herself, he would.

"Sam? Is she there?"

"Um – " He really didn't want Bernie to have to talk to her stepmother.

"Look, I know you are trying to protect her, but you don't have to worry. I have good news for her. Honest. I'll be good."

"Okay, but please be sensitive. She hasn't been able to shake this."

Sam walked the phone into the bedroom where Bernie lay twisting a piece of hair around her finger and staring into space. "Bernie?" he said lightly.

She saw the phone and immediately starting waving her hands back and forth in rejection.

"Sorry," Sam mouthed and handed it to her.

"Hello," she muttered into the receiver.

"Bernie! Honey, how are you?"

"Fine." Bernie's voice was flat and lifeless.

Her stepmother paused. "You don't sound fine."

Bernie sighed. "I'm not, actually. I feel pretty miserable. Sam's been trying to cheer me up."

"Well, good for him. You need it. We are so sorry. Have I told you how sorry we are?"

"Of course you have." In her amusement at this hundredth apology, a slight smile fleeted across Bernie's face. Sam caught it across the room and cheered considerably.

"I won't keep you long. I know how depressed you are. But, I have some good news for you. David, your rabbi, is coming to London."

Bernie sat up. "What? He is? To see me?"

"No, on his way to visit a friend in Israel. He has a stopover, so I was like, why not visit our Bernie? Check up on her. Cheer her up!"

"I don't think the rabbi is gonna help much."

"You never know, Bernie. He is a man of God."

She couldn't argue with that. "But what are we going to do with him? What do you do with a rabbi?"

"He's young like you. Take him out! Show him the sights!"

Bernie shrugged. "Okay. I'll show him a good time."

"That's our girl. You can talk to him about the ceremony as well. Nothing like focusing on the wedding to cheer a bride up."

Now, Bernie could definitely argue against that, but what was the point? She agreed to meet up with David the following weekend.

When she hung up the phone, she told Sam the plan.

"Next weekend?"

"Yep. Saturday."

"Next Saturday, as in England v Germany?"

Bernie nodded. She'd forgotten about the football game. "But he's our rabbi, Sam. What was I going to say? Thanks for flying thousands of miles and doing our ceremony, but no thanks? I'd rather watch the football? I'm practically related to him. He's my stepmother's cousin's son."

"Fine," he said. Then he scratched his head. "What does one do with a rabbi?"

Bernie scrunched her lips together. "Hmmm. Not sure. Take him to the pub to watch the football?"

Sam laughed. "You're kidding, right?"

Bernie wasn't kidding. On Saturday when they met David at his hotel, she laid out her plans. Surprisingly, he agreed. After all, men of God are people too. Some of them even like sports.

Of course, Sam and Bernie didn't just take him to the pub. They took him all over London during the day. David showed up on one of those perfect London summer days. Everyone in the city was out enjoying the sunshine and even smiling at perfect strangers. This seasonal disorder only occurred on days such as this. Londoners have perfected the art of personal space. Where else but here could you compress hundreds of people into a tube (literally The Tube) without any communication necessary (or desired) and still half of them manage to read a newspaper? You could be fooled into thinking London was a city of misanthropes, but you only have to stroll through any park on a sunny day and you will see them rollicking around with each other, just like normal folk.

Together with their rabbi, Sam and Bernie walked into the centre of town, past the fountains of Trafalgar Square down The Mall to Buckingham Palace and then for a stroll through St James Park. Bernie radiated pride in her new city and couldn't help but point out the gorgeous architecture, lush gardens and community feeling. Once in the park, Sam treated them all to an ice cream and they sat by the water to rest in the sun.

"It is so great to see you guys outside of the normal rabbi/ couple scenarios," David said.

"Like rabbi/couple ski trips? Or rabbi/couple wallpapering?" Bernie said.

He laughed. "I always meet with the couples, but never like this. Usually it's back at the temple, in some stuffy room. This is much better." He took a big bite from his ice cream cone. He smiled secretly. "I should say though, I have come with a message."

Bernie thought: *From God, please say it's from God.*

"Your stepmom told me about the situation with your mother."

Bernie groaned. If there was a message from God in this whole situation, it was a joke on her.

Sam said, "Yeah, well it has been tough for us. Well, really for Bernie." He put his arm around her shoulders and gave her a squeeze.

David finished his ice cream, crumpled the wrapping and put it aside. He seemed more serious now. "I may be stepping over my bounds, but I'm not just any rabbi, Bernie. I know your family. I'm practically part of it. I know we don't know each other that well, but I can't say I don't know anything about you. Suffice to say, your stepmother is," he looked up at the skies here, choosing his words carefully, "she's an expressive person, especially when it comes to this wedding."

Bernie shrugged. She would have been shocked if he didn't know. "I don't mind. To be honest, I think I'd rather you did know. This is the most profound ceremony we'll ever take part in; I'd rather you weren't just a nameless face. I'd prefer you knew some of our background."

"That's good. I'm glad to hear it." He sat up now, meaning business. "Now having heard everything, I think I have some advice. May I?"

Bernie nodded. She'd take anything just about now.

He continued. "You can't control what your mother does. Or what anyone does for that matter. You can only control your own choices. Now you two seem to me to be very much in love. True?"

Bernie instinctively looked at Sam and giggled. He took her hand and smiled back.

"Okay, then focus on that. Once the wedding is over, it doesn't matter how great or terrible everything looks, the flowers will wilt, the tuxedos will be returned, the guests will all go home. What will remain will be the two of you. In the end, that is what is important, that is what is gained from the day."

Bernie actually felt better. It *was* like a message from God, after all.

For the rest of the afternoon, the three of them talked over the ceremony. David helped them create exactly the type of service they felt would reflect their relationship. He did one other thing for them. David promised that no matter how many times any of her parents asked him, he would not reveal anything about the ceremony at all. Bernie knew this would drive her stepmother insane, but for her own sanity, she needed something that belonged only to Sam and herself, something that wasn't influenced by the opinions of others no matter how involved or not they were in the event.

Though she had no money to contribute, though she had no influence over the reception, Bernie clawed something back from the wedding. Her vows.

Later, they met up with some friends to watch the game. The pub was heaving. On the way over, Sam and Bernie prepped David with 'Football's Coming Home': English football's pop anthem. As their friends were already a bit tipsy, when the song came on and he joined in, everyone was thoroughly impressed. He followed this by buying the group a round and instantly became their favourite rabbi ever.

Maybe David grew tired of the endless references to 'The Rabbi', as in: does 'The Rabbi' need another drink; is 'The Rabbi' enjoying himself; or does 'The Rabbi' mind going out with a bunch of pissheads? After all, he was only a year older than Bernie and he had a first name. But if he did mind, he didn't show it.

Bernie hoped that when he stood up to lead their ceremony in a month's time, he would remember this night. She wanted him to see that she was more than this crazy wedding, or the pathetic sob story her stepmother, even with the best of intentions, made her out to be. Then again, maybe he could selectively subtract certain moments of the evening, so she was also more than just a drunken fool grinding on the pub dancefloor.

Wedding Truth No. 18

Your wedding will pass quickly, but your future with your husband will not.

If this Wedding Truth makes your heart sink a bit, stop now. End it. You wouldn't be the first to realise that you planned a wedding for the wrong reasons. Your boyfriend will hate you, true. But imagine how much he'll hate you in two years when you divorce him.

On the other hand, if this Wedding Truth makes you breathe a sigh of relief, then marriage is for you. This is only the first of many testing times for a couple. There will be more. If the notion of your future husband standing by your side through all the troubles life has in store calms you, you are making the right choice.

It is so easy to forget to look past the wedding itself. When my wedding became a war, it was so difficult, nay impossible, to see any way out besides going AWOL. I thought if I wanted to marry my boyfriend, I had to go through with everything, even after my mother disowned me.

Hopefully, your wedding will never be so complicated. But sometimes, even discussions over what canapés to serve can seem like battles. Remember, canapés will make no difference to your marriage. On the other hand, those vows you take are the most important part of the day, and they are your own. What a relief when the rabbi told us we could choose them ourselves and no one, not even him, could do it for us.

I felt empowered again. I felt like a bride.

Chapter Eighteen: Let The Wedding Negotiations Begin

"Your mother wants to meet," Bernie's dad said ominously over the phone. It was only two weeks before Bernie was meant to fly back home for the wedding. She hadn't heard a word from her mother since that last phone call.

Stunned Bernie replied, "She called you?"

He fired back, "No, of course she didn't call me. My wife is receiving orders from your fiancé, Bernie. Apparently I am the link that ties you and your mother together." Her father sounded annoyed, "I can't say I like how he spoke to her, but I tried anyway. Besides, it worked. She wants to see you now."

"She does?"

"Indeed. Shocking, isn't it? Maybe she doesn't hate you after all. You're off the list."

"The list?"

"You know, the list of traitors. I had the number one slot until a couple of weeks back. Now I'm back and you are a piddly second place." Bernie could hear him shuffle some papers. "Don't get too jealous. It's not like the World Series you know. It's not a race you want to win. So?" His voice rose with this dangling question.

"So what?"

"So are you going to see her?"

"What do you think I should do?"

"Well, after Sam yelled at my wife about arranging it for you, I would hope you would go. But, don't do it for me. Think about yourself. You only have one mother and yours wants to speak with you. Hear her out."

Her father was a man of simple truths and this one struck home. She felt her resilience fading. "Okay, I'll be out at the end of the month for the wedding preparations. Tell her I will meet with her then."

"You could tell her yourself," he said leadingly.

She smirked, "I thought you were 'the tie that binds us'."

He laughed, "Okay, okay. I'll tell you what I'll do. I'll get your sister to do it."

"Very brave."

He laughed. "See you at the end of the month."

* * *

When Bernie packed this last final time for Detroit before the wedding, Sam offered a few words of advice. "Drink. Drink heavily and drink heartily."

"Is that your only advice? Do you ever think you are turning me into an alcoholic?"

As if in answer, he produced a bottle of champagne. "Let's send you off in style, shall we?"

Bernie smiled for the first time in days and helped herself, heavily and heartily. The following day she would fly home and the day after that, she would discover if her relationship with her mother would survive the wedding.

* * *

Bernie arrived at her mother's designated meeting point late on purpose. Witnessing her mother's grand entrance did not appeal to her. She lingered, sweltering in her father's car, borrowed for just this occasion, the Michigan summer heat and humidity closing in on her stationary position. The building rested in a concrete parking lot, adorned with scatterings of bushes and plant life. It was grey like the lot, its windows covered in those reflective mirrored seals that are so popular in faceless office blocks.

Inside, her mother waited in her psychologist's office. She

insisted Bernie meet her there as opposed to the house, as if she wanted a witness in case Bernie attacked her. At least, that was what Bernie thought at the time. Perhaps Bernie's mother just realised that they needed a negotiator. Even Bernie would have agreed with that.

Bernie slumped into the office, where they were already waiting. She marvelled at their composure. The therapist sat relaxed, reclining in his seat, legs long and lean in front of him, one tucked under the ankle of the other, hands clasped at his waist. He kept his beard trimmed, wore a v neck sweater, white pressed shirt and a novelty Bugs Bunny tie. Cheap, local, modernist art dotted the walls. On the desk next to him sat a plaque: "A dream is a rainbow where each colour combines to show the light of our true nature. Your inner light will lead you to your pot of gold." Leaning against this plaque was a dusty Freud ceramic miniature, holding an open notebook in his hand and a pencil in his mouth, finished with a caricaturist comedy expression.

Bernie's mother sat on one end of a purple leather couch. She raised her head when Bernie appeared, pursed her lips and made an uncomfortable show of greeting her by rising and lightly placing her arms on Bernie's shoulders, distancing her body but kissing her on the cheek. Inside, Bernie reacted as if an elephant had stomped on her face. Her mother returned to the couch. She sat poised and elegant as always. In comparison, Bernie felt a mess, inside and out. Rather than be engulfed by lavender cushions, Bernie plopped herself down in the armchair adjacent.

"Hello, Bernadette. My name is Bill."

"Hello," Bernie said cagily.

"We are gathered here today to see if we might join you two together in a healthy relationship." The wedding jargon did not go unnoticed by Bernie, though her mother and Bill seemed oblivious. "Perhaps, as she asked you here today, your mother would like to begin by saying why she has invited you."

Her mother nodded as if on cue from some grand script. "Thank you, Bill." She turned to Bernie. "Bernadette. I am your mother. I have looked after you and watched you grow into a young lady. I believe that you have disrespected the role I have played in your life. And by refusing to apologise, to take responsibility for your actions, I am at a loss as to what to do." Here she looked pleadingly at Bill then dropped her eyes.

"And you, Bernadette? How do you respond to this emotional turmoil your mother is experiencing?"

Bernie saw immediately how the cards were being dealt. This wasn't a negotiation. This was a pitched battle against her. "First of all," Bernie said firmly, "I did not put my mother through anything. Whatever she is experiencing is self-inflicted. She disowned me."

"Are you listening to your mother, Bernadette?" He continued methodically as if she hadn't spoken. "I think if you recognised her pain you both could start to move forward. She is calling out to you. Turn to her. Speak to her."

Bernie stiffened in defence, but turned to her mother directly. She spoke in the even tones of the psychologist, tempering herself in hopes of breaching her mother's defences. "Mother, you abandoned me. You left me. You have done such damage to our relationship that I don't know if I will ever be able to trust you again."

Her mother answered in the same tone. "Trust is something that must be earned Bernadette. It is not something I have in you."

"Mother, I'm speaking of my trust in you."

"Until you recognise the pain you inflicted here," her mother looked to her psychologist for encouragement before continuing, "we can never mend our differences."

Bernadette wondered why she had come here today. Her mother only wanted more of the same. They would never see eye to eye.

"Bernadette, try to see things from your mother's point of view. Feel her pain for a moment."

Bernadette could take no more. Her eyes started welling up again for the hundredth time in the past month. "No offence Bill," she began, "but you are my mother's psychologist. She pays you. She's seen you for years. I haven't. This all seems a little one-sided to me."

"I can assure you…" he began.

Bernadette held up her hand. "If you would give me a moment," she said, tears now forming tiny rivers down her shirt. "Mother, I've come here today to make amends with you. We are never going to see eye to eye. I will always remember what you have done and I don't think I will ever forgive you…"

"But Bernadette," she said.

"Wait." Even Bernie needed a moment here before continuing. "Consider that after everything, I still showed up here today. Even though we disagree on the reasons why things turned out this way, I love you and I want you at my wedding. I've made the first step and I'm afraid that is all I can offer you right now." Bernie stood up. Her body felt dull and heavy. She longed to hold her mother, but she reached for a tissue off Bill's desk instead. "Do you want to come to my wedding?" she asked.

"Do you want me there?" her mother, said sounding genuine as opposed to scripted for the first time.

Bernie answered her honestly. "Yes."

Bill looked perplexed, but he couldn't help but interject. "I sense a strong bond between the two of you. If you could just sit down Bernadette and try to reconnect with…"

"Bill," Bernie's mother said without turning to him, "really, it's okay." She kept her eyes on her daughter. "I will accept your invitation, but I have one condition."

"Fine," Bernie said. She would accept anything at this point, from flower arrangements to dessert menus. All that mattered was her mother at the wedding and some hope of a later resolution between them.

"I'll come to the ceremony, but I won't stay for your stepmother's party. She arranged everything and I won't have it rubbed in my face. When the ceremony ends, I will leave along with my guests."

Bernie didn't pause for a second. She held out her hand, her mother grasped it and they shook on it, like men finalising a challenging business deal. They didn't feel like mother and daughter, but maybe because of this moment someday they would.

Bernie had one final thought for her mother before she turned to leave. "See you at the wedding."

Wedding Truth No. 19

When life gives you lemons, make lemonade.

When my mom taught me that maxim little did she know I would use it to comfort myself while dealing with this mess.

Many people have asked me how I could forgive my mother. For me, it was never a question.

I reminded myself that my mother is more than just a woman at my wedding. She was the comforting voice when I came home crying from school. She was the soothing hand on my fevered brow. She was the one who kept me in check as a teenager; drove me to endless drum, drama, voice, ballet lessons; sat with me on long Sunday afternoons encouraging me to create my own little art and crafts masterpieces out of noodles and glitter.

And yes, she was also the one who went mental during my engagement. But even at the time, I knew it stemmed in part from the fear that once her daughter left, the opportunity to build new memories might go with her.

Everyone, from the bride down, is more than their role on one wedding day. My mother is no exception.

She handed me some lemons. I made lemonade. I love her.

Chapter Nineteen: Bridal Breakdown

Bernie left the therapist's office in tears, she drove her father's car in tears, she arrived at the restaurant to meet her father in tears. She should have felt better, reconciled but she didn't. She should have envisioned a future with her mother but she didn't. She pulled the rearview mirror down to examine the damage. Her eyes were swollen, her hair was dishevelled, her cheeks, lips and nose puffy.

"You look like shit," she said to her reflection.

Bernie called her father from the car park on the mobile phone that he had let her borrow for the duration of her stay.

"Hey!" he called into the phone, "Where are you?"

"Um, in the parking lot."

"The what? What do you mean? Has there been an accident?"

"No."

"Are you hurt?"

"No, well yes. I'm upset. I just left my meeting with Mom," she reminded him.

"Oh God," he sounded concerned. "I'm sorry. Didn't go well, then?"

"Well, she said she'll come to the ceremony but not the reception."

"Well, that's an improvement isn't it? Isn't it?"

Bernie sobbed as an answer.

"Okay, look, your stepmom's in the restroom. I'll fill her in. Come inside, it will be okay. We can talk it over after we eat."

"Dad, I keep crying. I can't come in."

"Come in already. We've been waiting here. It's one o'clock. We're hungry. It will be okay."

"Dad?"

"What?"

Bernie started to blubber. "Do you think she'll hate me forever?"

"No, honey. She'll see the light eventually. Don't worry. Besides, she'll always hate me more. You have that to comfort you."

Bernie giggled despite herself. "Thanks Dad."

"No prob. Now listen, are you going to sit in that car all day? This is stupid. Come inside and have some food."

"Okay."

"Alright then, good, see you in a minute."

Bernie clicked the phone shut and set to cleaning up her face. She breathed deeply and fanned her red eyes. She tried to think happy thoughts. Ice cream. Little puppies. Sam. She started tearing up again.

"Stop this," she said to her reflection. "Sam will be here tomorrow and you can cry to him all you want then. Got it?" Inside she answered, *got it*.

Bernie dragged her fingers through her hair, took a few more deep breaths for good measure and walked into the restaurant.

"Oh, hello, Boo-Boo!" Bernie's stepmother cried from across the restaurant. She raced up and hugged her. "Your Dad just told me. Don't you worry about a thing. You know we love you, right? Right?"

"Right," Bernie said, managing a small smile. More than anything in the world right now, she wanted to crawl under a duvet and sleep or sob or both.

"Come here," her stepmother said grabbing Bernie's hand in her own bejewelled one. "Hi, Melvin!" she called out to someone as she dragged Bernie to the table. "How's the ulcer? Good! Good! Tell Selma we said hi!" She turned back to face Bernie as they walked, "He has a terrible ulcer. Causes all kinds of problems for their marriage that I would never dare speak to you about. Oh! Here we are!"

Bernie's father got up and hugged her. "Don't worry honey," he said kissing her cheek and hugging her again, "It will all be over soon."

They all slid into the booth and Bernie looked through the menu. It all looked revolting. Thoughts of duvets and pillows floated seductively through her head.

"What d'ya want?" her father said. "Hamburger? You want breakfast? You know they do breakfast all day here."

"Yeah, that sounds good. Maybe an egg and hashbrowns."

"Good choice." Her father raised his arm and shouted to a waitress, "Hey! Can we get some service over here and some coffee. My daughter needs a coffee."

The waitress scooted over with a steaming mug to take their order. Once she was gone, her stepmother began.

"So! We thought it would be great if after brunch we went and did the cake tasting."

Bernie groaned. "Do we need to? How many flavours of cake can there be?"

"Oh my God, like 200! And every single one delicious."

Bernie felt her insides collapse. "Well, to be honest, I'd rather just wait until tomorrow. I'm really wedding-ed out today."

"Tomorrow? No way, honey," she said. "We'll do it today. You'll love it. I've picked out the best cake maker in Detroit. He does all the best weddings. He's a total asshole, I mean a real son of a bitch, but his cakes! They are so gorgeous."

"Really, I would prefer to wait until tomorrow. Sam will be in then, and he can go with us."

"Oh, Sam doesn't care a single bit about cake."

"He might," Bernie said weakly.

"Give me a break, Bernadette," she said. "Sam does not care one hoot about cake flavours."

Bernie thought of how little Sam was given a chance to voice his opinion in regards to the wedding. She felt her resolve grow. She would achieve this. This one thing. He liked sweets. It was important. She said, "But it would be nice if he could be here to choose them. I mean, it's one day. What can it hurt?"

"And there will be nothing to choose after today? Come on, Bernadette. There are going to be a million things to do after today when he is in. When are you going to do the tasting? Tomorrow right after he arrives? When he is jet-lagged? The morning of the rehearsal dinner? I mean really."

Bernie looked to her father who was reading his paper silently during this whole exchange. "Dad?"

He looked at her over the sports section. "Why don't you just go? It will be easier for everyone."

"But don't you think Sam – "

"Bernadette," her stepmother said. "Now stop being silly."

Bernie slapped her hands down on the table. "I'm not being silly! Cake is very important to us! I want Sam to taste it and he will taste it and he wants to taste it and we don't get anything we want for this wedding so he can at least taste a cake!"

Her stepmother looked at her sternly from across the formica table. "Bernadette, calm down."

"Well, how am I supposed to get through to anyone!"

"Bernadette, that's enough!" Now her father was getting in on the argument. He whipped his newspaper to the side.

"All I want is for someone to let Sam taste the cake!" Tears were streaming down her face now. She should never have come in. She should have gone home. "Sam deserves cake! And so do I! We love cake and no one is going to take that away from us! The cake flavour is very, very, very important to us! " Bernie reached into her pocket and flung her father's car keys and phone at him. "Here you go! I'm leaving."

Bernadette raced out of the restaurant, tears and snot streaming down her face. She ran from the door across the car park and on to the sidewalk adjacent to the main road. And then she started to walk. And walk. She huffed and wiped her dripping eyes. She swore under her breath. She probably looked close to insanity.

Bernadette carried on like this for about five minutes before she calmed down. Then she took a look around her. She was in the suburbs. Where was she going to go? She turned around. She was at least a half-hour walk from anywhere. In the suburbs there is no public transport. She had no phone. She had no car.

"Real smart," she muttered to herself. She fell to her knees behind a sign announcing a new subdivision. She rested her back against its wooden stake, pulled her knees in to her chest and wrapped her arms around them as she gathered her thoughts.

What am I doing? was the first thought. *Where do I think I'm going?* was the second. *Does Sam even like cake?* was the third.

Bernadette stood up and brushed her clothes off and began the long walk back to the restaurant, her pride dragging behind her. All cried out, she surveyed the restaurant before entering. Her father was nowhere to be seen but her stepmother was still there. She was pacing the length of the diner, speaking to Bernie's father through her mobile phone. Bernie took a deep breath and walked inside.

"Oh!" her stepmother cried out pointing at Bernie across the restaurant. "She's here! She's back!" She snapped her phone shut and rushed over to Bernadette. "Oh, honey," her stepmother cried. "We are so sorry. I am so sorry. You're about to have a total breakdown and I'm talking about cake."

"No, it's okay. I know the cake isn't important. I'm just upset about my mother."

"I totally, totally understand."

At that moment her father came through the doors. "Bernadette! You came back. I've been looking everywhere for you. Are you okay?"

"Yes. I'm sorry. I think I'm just letting everything get to me these days."

"Well, you should lighten up. It's just cake." He came over and gave her a big hug. "Don't worry about it."

Bernadette sat back down at the table she had run from just minutes ago. Her stepmother clasped her hand from across the table. "I'll tell you what, after this meal I'll take you over to Jill Steinberg. She's a regressive therapist."

"What, you mean she'll hypnotise me and regress me back to the 18th century? I don't get it."

"Oh, don't worry. I'm too scared to have her do it to me either. No, you don't have to have her regress you. I'm just telling you that because she is a world-class therapist. Bernadette, you almost had a total breakdown there. I think you need to go speak to someone."

153

"Oh, it's okay. I'll be fine."

"No way! I won't hear of it. You are going."

"No, really, I'll be fine. Besides I can't afford a therapist."

Bernie's stepmother raised her hands in exasperation. "Are you listening to this?" she said to Bernie's father. "Bernadette, I will pay for it. You need help."

Bernie looked over at her father. "Can't hurt," he said.

Bernie shrugged. "Okay, fine. I'll go." Maybe the regressive therapist would bring her back to a time a year back when she thought a wedding was a good idea and mentally shift that idea. Or maybe she would regress her back to the 18th century and then leave her there.

"Good, because I've already arranged it," her stepmother said. "I called when you ran away."

"Thanks."

"And then I thought we could go cake tasting."

Bernie looked up at her stepmother and then her father. They were serious. "And then we'll go cake tasting," Bernie repeated.

Her stepmother clapped her hands together in glee. "Oh, good! You'll love it."

* * *

The therapist didn't have to regress her. Actually, in comparison to what Bernadette expected, Jill Steinberg seemed pretty sensible. Her office was done up in muted colours, the seats comfortable and the tissue box offered up first thing "just in case" as she said.

Two therapists in under three hours, Bernie thought. *This must be a record.*

Bernie cleared her throat. "Er, my stepmother thought this would be a good idea. You know I live in another country. I'm not, um, going to be a recurring patient." *Unless I am in another life,* Bernie thought to herself with amusement.

"Don't worry," Jill said, "your stepmother filled me in a bit. Just tell me whatever you want to get off your chest and I'll see if I can help at all."

Bernie leaned forward. "First of all, I just want to say that you know my stepmother and I know she is paying for this session. Also, you work and, I'm assuming, live in this area, you might know my mother."

"Yes…"

"I am really, really going to hold you to that confidentiality agreement."

Jill smiled. "No problem."

So Bernie spilled. And spilled. All the stories of the wedding poured out of her. Now that she didn't need to bottle the stories up anymore, she didn't cry or grow angrier or more frustrated. Jill listened patiently, asked gentle questions and shook her head.

When Bernie finished, Jill sat there in amazement for quite a while. "I'm just stunned," she said. "I've never heard such a story before."

"But what should I do?"

"I have no idea." Well, this was refreshing at least. Bernie didn't know what to do either. "I will say a couple things though," Jill continued, "First, your mother wouldn't be acting like this if she didn't love you. People don't get upset and react in such extremes to things they don't care about. And second, you can at least comfort yourself that it will all be over soon. Keep reminding yourself of that."

Bernie nodded. This all made sense to her.

"One more thing," Jill said.

"Yeah?"

"I've got to know what happens. Will you let me know? You could write me a letter, or something?"

Bernie grimaced a bit inside. Her life was now just a titillating story.

Wedding Truth No. 20

Insanity is a natural accompaniment to weddings.

If you find yourself in the position I found myself in that day (at a local diner, shouting at the top of my lungs how important cake flavourings were) take care. You are going into Total Mental Collapse. It's not an official condition, but it is one that most brides will experience at some point in the planning.

There will be many, many people who won't understand why you are getting so worked up over cake flavourings. There will be many, many people who think it is only a choice between chocolate or vanilla. Who think: "My God, how hard can it be?" Or even: "Who cares?"

They are right.

When cake flavourings become so important that you lose all self-control in a hamburger joint, you need help.

You will read bridal magazines and books that comfort you with the thought that actually cake flavourings are important. They will tell you that your temper tantrum is justified due to the stress of the wedding. Poor you, etc.

These people are wrong.

I can not stress enough. Cake flavourings are not important. Your sanity is.

Finally, if this message still isn't getting through, some help: Choose vanilla. No one hates vanilla and you have the added bonus of it matching your dress. Besides, most people will be too stuffed with food or drunk by the time dessert arrives to care.

Okay? Now, start breathing again.

Chapter Twenty: The Eleventh Hour

This time when he flew to the States, to avoid the flight
fiasco pre-engagement, Sam made sure he took a non-stop flight.
Nothing would get in the way of him joining Bernie. She could
barely suppress her thrill on his arrival. At the airport, he wrapped
his arms around her and, not for the first time, she felt that warm,
comfortable security that only he gave her.

Sam kissed the top of her head. "You okay, honey?" he asked.

"Yep," she smiled, taking his hand and leading him out of the
airport, "Now I am. I feel just fine."

They spent two days in Detroit in final negotiations about the
little details of the wedding, before driving five hours to Toronto,
Canada to pick up two friends from England, Clare and her boyfriend
William.

Their one night in Toronto was spent roaming the city, hitting
a few pubs and coercing each other up the CN tower, the world's
tallest building. It was terrifyingly high, but a few drinks later in the
bar, and they all felt they were coping quite well. On the way out of
the building, giddy from the height and the drinks, Bernie took the
boys' arms and someone who overheard their banter shouted as
they went past, "Hey, it's S-Club 7!"

"Did you hear that?" Clare cried with absolute glee. "We are
practically celebrities and we aren't even in the States yet. I love
Canada!" She started belting out the S Club theme song and doing
a little gig in the street. Clare was slightly drunk.

The next morning, no longer celebrities, the four friends hit a diner on the way out of town and began the long drive back to Detroit. William talked non-stop from the back, listing endless useless facts about Canada.

"Did you know?" he said. "Detroit is the only border in the US where you go South to enter Canada?"

No one minded. Bernie loved conversations that leaned towards empty chatter as opposed to debates over appropriate wedding table settings. She would have gladly stayed in that car forever, gleaning more information about Canada than she could have ever hoped for and been quite satisfied.

As they approached the border, Bernie said, "Let's not have any trouble today, boys. Just say you are visiting. Don't mention the wedding, okay?"

They all agreed. After Bernie's deportation from Britain, she took no chances. She had no idea how the border police would react to Sam entering the country to marry her.

They joined the long line of cars approaching the border and finally the border itself. Bernie rolled down her window.

"Where are you coming from?" the woman asked.

"Toronto, but I live in Detroit," Bernie said cheerfully.

The woman wasn't the cheerful type. "And why were you in Toronto?"

"I was picking up these guys. They're staying with me for a few days. It was cheaper to fly into Canada."

"And where are they from?"

"Britain."

The woman cleared her throat, throwing her voice down two octaves. "Pull to the left. Park. Passports out. Car registration out. Enter the main building for interviews."

Bernie shrugged and pulled forward. Everyone else got out while she rifled through the glovebox for her car registration papers. Clutching all her documentation, she met them inside.

Officer Hindenburg stood behind the counter eyeing up the group. They stood tense, in silence. Clare looked frightened. William gripped her waist protectively. Bernie nervously took Sam's hand.

Officer Hindenburg placed each passport open in front of him, lined up in order of appearance. He gripped the edge of the counter separating him from their group. Officer Hindenburg stood before them like an immigration gladiator, a border soldier, more than a mere public servant. He looked like the type of man who lived for these moments. He didn't seem to notice the heat of the summer. He ignored the sweat dripping from under his tight uniform. Around his waist where his belt cinched his flesh, under his arms and down his front, a growing stain of sweat turned his beige shirt a deep, rusty brown. Glasses emphasised his bulging eyes. Now and again he pulled them down to scan a passport and then slid them back up his nose to huff in disgust. Several minutes into this routine, he turned to Bernie.

"So, what's this I hear about a wedding?"

Her heart dropped. She felt it fluttering faintly to her bowels. In the moments she was separated from them, one of them must have slipped. She didn't blame whoever it was, she was terrified herself. "My wedding?" she eked out.

"Yep. The one and the same. You got a special visa for your future husband?"

"No, I called. They said I didn't need one."

"Well, that's a lie right there young lady." His voice clipped with a slight southern drawl. "If you did indeed call up as you claim, you would know that the US of A does not allow foreigners to enter the country to marry its citizens without a visa."

Bernie took a deep breath and tried not to cry. Would Officer Hindenburg turn Sam away? Send him home? "I assure you officer, I did call. I called several times actually, and each time, when I explained that I would be moving back to the UK with him, they said it was fine. No visa."

Officer Hindenburg obviously felt the need to launch into a grand scale interrogation. He didn't hesitate to hammer away at Bernie's story or confidence. "Lies," he barked. "Keep telling them. It will make my job all the more easier."

Bernie broke. Tears streamed down her face. "You can check. I have a job teaching in a London school in September. It's all lined up. You may not believe me, sir, but I called many times. I know the problems people can run into at the border. I wanted to avoid them. Please – "

Officer Hindenburg huffed. "True or not, you still have no visa. I'm going to have to speak to my superiors."

William tried speaking on Bernie's behalf. "Excuse me officer, if I may just interject. Bernie is telling – "

"Am I the officer here or are you!" Hindenburg bellowed. "Interrupt these interrogations again and I'll have you arrested. Do I make myself clear?"

"Perfectly," William whimpered.

Officer Hindenburg pointed to interview rooms to the side. "You," he said pointing to Sam, "Room 1. You," he said this time pointing to Clare, "Room 2," and so on until they were all separated. Bernie walked like a zombie into her room. Bars crossed the tiny window, too high for her to see out anyway. She sobbed uncontrollably, certain this time would mirror her original deportation.

While the minutes passed, her father and family were waiting for them all to arrive. Tonight he planned on taking them all out, introducing himself to her London friends. Without any way to contact him or Sam next door, Bernie lost all hope.

Finally, over an hour later, Officer Hindenburg opened the door. Her friends and Sam waited outside, looking shocked but ready to go. Sam flashed his passport at her. "It's all okay," he said.

Officer Hindenburg said nothing to her. He didn't say goodbye, or explain how he came to his decision to let them go. He turned his back to them and began filling out paperwork.

Bernie didn't quite believe it. "He's letting you through? It's okay?"

Sam led her outside. "All fine," he said. "Seems like it was just a slow day for Officer Hindenburg."

Bernie gasped and hugged Sam. Almost deported. She held his face and kissed it firmly. "Thank God," she said gratefully, "I couldn't go through with this wedding on my own."

Sam laughed, "It would be challenging without a groom."

"At this point, nothing would surprise me."

After calling her father from a nearby payphone to explain the delay, the four climbed back in the car and travelled over the Ambassador Bridge, which links Canada to the USA. The Detroit River passed beneath them, and Bernie hoped the worst of her troubles had now completely washed away with its currents.

* * *

Bernie spent the next couple of days settling Sam's family and their friends into their hotels and showing them around town. The days turned into a whirlwind of restaurants and historic drives.

Finally, the night before the wedding arrived. Her father and stepmother hosted a rehearsal dinner for all the out-of-town guests at an Italian restaurant. Both her father and stepmother beamed with pride as she walked them around introducing them to everyone. The celebratory mood of the group enthused Bernie. She was pleased to see that Clare and her boyfriend were laughing and eating with Anne and the rest of her Michigan friends. Sam's parents were made welcome by all her relatives. Everyone seemed to be getting along and looking forward to the wedding. She let the stress of the last few days, and even months, fall away in the rapture of being with her family and friends which, in the end, was all she really wanted from the wedding to begin with.

After they had all consumed an obscene amount of pizza and garlic bread, Beth motioned for Bernie to start saying her goodbyes. The restaurant staff were loitering nervously, clocking the time and the growing throng of customers waiting to be seated. Bernie pulled her father aside before speaking to anyone else. "Dad," she said, "I'd like to meet you tomorrow for one final breakfast between father and daughter before I become a married woman." She thought he'd jump at the offer, but instead he looked a bit perplexed so she continued, "I know it's the wedding day, but I don't have to be at my hair appointment till 10.30, you could pick me up at 9 am. Dad?"

"Um," he faltered. She thought it would be so nice, time to themselves before the wedding, but he acted uncertain. Finally he said, "Sure, sure honey. No prob. Call me in the morning and I'll pick you up." He kissed her on the cheek. "See you tomorrow for the big day."

Bernie watched as he rushed off to say his goodbyes and wondered what the big deal was.

Beth clambered up to her. "Say your goodbyes, Bernie. We have plans." Her voice was unusually high and she was giggling wickedly.

"Plans?" Bernie said nervously.

"Oh, yeah. Big plans. Hurry up."

Nothing like a sister to make a bride feel comfortable the night before her wedding.

Wedding Truth No. 21

It's the week of the wedding. Anything can happen.

Hopefully, you won't watch your fiancé almost get deported like I did, but I guarantee something cataclysmic will happen the week of the wedding. Not to panic you, but here's just a couple of things that happened to me: I forgot to pick up my marriage licence and I forgot to collect my relatives from the airport. Only two of the most important things for your wedding: the certificate that legitimises the wedding and family who witness it.

I remembered both these things at the exact same moment and had an instantaneous, total meltdown. I squealed my car off the road and into one of the thousands of shopping malls that line Michigan suburbs. I pelted into a diner in tears, sobbing and screaming for a phone directory and a telephone. Maybe they feared me. Maybe they thought I'd just been in a major accident. Certainly, I appeared less than sane. Some pimply teenager took pity on me and gave me what I asked for.

Thankfully, the relatives were collected, be it a bit late. But even more incredible, my best friend woke up at the crack of dawn (a near miracle in itself) to drive to the State of Michigan registry department the following morning. An angel at the offices for the State of Michigan opened the registry on the weekend to save my wedding and hand over the marriage certificate. Bless you, Angel of the State of Michigan.

Complications will arise the week of your wedding and you too will feel like a miracle happens when they are solved. But remember, or try to if you're not in hysterics like I was, they will be solved.

Chapter Twenty one: Last Night in Singledom

Following the rehearsal dinner, Bernie stood outside the restaurant waiting for her sister and the inevitable "plan" Beth had spoke of. Bernie tried to assure herself that her sister had her best interests at heart, but it was difficult. Revenge is a word that close sisters save for just such occasions. Bernie stuffed Beth down many a bed crack in their youth; tonight could just well be Beth's night to get her own back.

Keeping to tradition, she and Sam would spend the night apart; her with her best friends and sister, him out with all the guys who'd flown into town. The men, including Sam, checked into a hotel earlier that day, where the following night, he and Bernie would spend their first night together as a married couple.

Sam came up behind Bernie and wrapped his arms around her. Bernie turned and poked Sam's chest with a manicured fingernail, prepped earlier that day for the wedding. "I know you are going to have a couple of beers tonight," she began, watching his eyes dive immediately into a roll, "but I swear, if you show up hungover tomorrow, after all we've been through, I will never forgive you." She felt cruel, but then, sometimes the truth is better. Hungover at the wedding was not an option for Bernie.

She needn't have worried. "I'm more nervous than you, Bernie. I'm setting two alarms and getting a wake up call. I imagine I'll be the first in bed tonight."

Bernie sighed, "I'm not trying to be a monster. I just don't think I will survive anymore disasters. I want one thing out of this wedding to be a success. Just one day, that's all I'm asking for."

He lifted her chin with his hand and kissed her gently. "You got it, honey." He smiled, "I'll limit myself to ten pints. Honest. I'll just do the Impossible Dream tonight and then right to bed."

Bernie smacked him laughing, "Sam!"

"I'm kidding!" He mocked blocking her punches with fright, "Don't hurt the groom! I can't look bruised tomorrow."

Bernie gave him one last squeeze as Anne's car screeched up to the entrance. Her sister and Clare were piled in with her. Bernie felt more emotional than she thought she would. When she broke away from Sam, she started welling up like they would never see each other again. She told herself to get a grip.

As soon as she climbed in the back and clicked her seatbelt into place, Anne peeled out of the restaurant parking lot. The radio blasted. All the girls cheered.

In the front, Beth turned the music down briefly, "Anne, do you mind driving up by Twelve Oaks Mall? It doesn't close for another two hours and I want to see if I can get a few accessories for tomorrow." She swivelled around, "No one minds, do you?"

Clare shook her head, but Bernie was a bit miffed. "Is this 'The Plan'? Shop Bernie to death? Do we have to?" she huffed. "I'm so stressed. I just want to take a bath."

"Oh, come on," Beth said, "it will do you some good. You can't just mope around Anne's house all night. It's better to walk around a bit, take your mind off the big day."

Bernie didn't agree, but as the other girls were all chirping in agreement, she resigned herself to a last minute shopping excursion. The girls giggled over the music for the remainder of the ride, while Bernie sat, quiet in the back, reflecting on the big event tomorrow.

How did she get to this point? Months of agony, her relationship with her mother in tatters, a British husband, a new career, a life overseas – her life was nothing like what she imagined it would be a couple years back. She felt both terrified and thrilled.

Bernie thought back to those first days when she met Sam. How they were the only ones on their course with rooms in a hall on the opposite side of the campus. How they used to walk the long journey back from class together through wooded paths, long before they ever kissed or even conceived of a moment when they'd be a couple. How they argued over politics or literature or who owed whom a pint. How everyone used to tease them that they were going out when they weren't and then how it seemed so natural when they did.

Bernie remembered all the kind things he'd done for her even before they went out together. Saving half his meals for her when she was too broke to buy one for herself. Leaving her the key to his room so when he went home to Wales for the weekend, she could watch his telly. Coming back from a trip to the States to find he had set out a little saucepan with a can of mushroom soup and a cola because he anticipated she'd be hungry but would not have the energy to even think about what to eat.

Bernie smiled in the car. She was a sentimental fool. And a lucky one at that.

The girls continued to sing, oblivious to Bernie's romantic flashbacks. Anne's voice blared the loudest. She squealed the car into the Twelve Oaks Mall car park, crying out, "Here we are, ladies!"

Like most American malls, it hardly looked inviting: bleak, brown and enormous. Bernie felt the crushing pressure of being trapped in a sea of tacky accessories and endless clothes racks. But for some reason, the other girls saw it as their Shangri-La.

Beth whipped around to stare at Bernie. "Oh! Here we are! Excited?"

"Thrilled," Bernie responded in what she hoped was as dull a tone as possible.

"I thought we'd go to all the major department stores first, then hit all the jewellery stores inside to do a comparison," Beth rallied.

"Sounds awesome!" Anne cried.

Bernie wondered if she'd been hijacked onto the mall's personal cheerleading squad.

"This is so great," Clare said, her voice faltering. "Shopping malls. It's so, um, American. I've always wanted to do this. Um, a lifelong dream. I'm totally gung-ho."

Bernie looked at her in amazement. What was she on about? Then just as suddenly, something clicked in Bernie's head. British women don't get "gung-ho" about anything.

"Lifelong dream? The mall?" Bernie exclaimed. "Are you taking the piss?"

"The what?" Beth said, turning around again. "I didn't get that. Does someone need the toilet?"

Bernie's frustration grew. "I meant, are you joking?"

Clare smiled, "Yeah. Actually we are."

"What?" Bernie was totally baffled.

Anne swerved the car off the mall's internal road network and onto a long driveway. The road wound away from the mall and off around a lake.

"What's going on?" Bernie said. The girls laughed raucously. Bernie gripped the sides of her seat like a vice. "Girls? This isn't funny. You do know I'm getting married tomorrow."

"Abso-████████-lutely," Anne said. "That's exactly why we arranged this." At that moment, the car swerved off into the lot of a swank hotel.

Beth said, "All suites. Already arranged. Packed your stuff earlier. It's in the back."

"It is?" Bernie said in disbelief.

Anne pulled into a parking space and turned around. "It is," she said. "Now come on. Why don't we go up and see your room."

Bernie the zombie stepped out of the car and followed the girls up the stairs.

"I already checked in for you on the way to the rehearsal dinner. And I hope you don't mind, but I'm going to be staying the night too," Beth said.

"But what about tomorrow," Bernie said in a panic.

"Not a problem," Beth said. "The hairdresser is in the mall and I made arrangements with Dad already to drop you off at the diner at nine for breakfast. It's right across the street."

Bernie realised now why her father seemed so put out by her request for breakfast the following day. He must have known about this.

The girls reached the room and Beth handed over the key. "Your room, Madame Bernadette..." she said.

Bernie clicked open the door and stepped in. The room was gorgeous. There were two beds and a separate lounge with its own fridge and kitchen table. Bernie opened the fridge. It was full of beer.

"Wow," was all she could think to say.

"We thought you might need a drink tonight," Clare said.

Then in unison the girls said with strong nasal undertones, "... but I swear, if you show up hungover tomorrow..."

"Yes. Ha-ha. Very funny," Bernie said sarcastically. But she was laughing. She reached in and cracked open a beer for each of them. "A toast," she said, "to great friends and a future of laughter like this."

"Hear, hear!" they all said and took a long swig each.

Wedding Truth No. 22

Eat before your wedding. Forget the wedding diet. If you haven't lost it by now, there isn't hope.

I'm one for big breakfasts before brave leaps off cliffs, or, as it's called in this case, taking the plunge. Americans don't do a lot of great food, but they do cook great breakfasts. For this reason alone, consider America for your wedding.

I imagine many brides feel sick before their weddings. I felt a bit giddy myself. I didn't eat much, but I did take advantage of the situation to sample blueberry pancakes, hashbrowns, scrambled eggs, a bagel, melon and two cups of coffee. Sounds like a lot. Okay, it was a lot. But my Dad was there to help me out.

Following this I was dropped at the mall where some girl lacquered my hair into a totally unnatural shape and then stuck it to my skull with sharp bobby pins. Later I discovered the hairdo defied gravity entirely. Following the ceremony, and unable to endure the entrapment anymore, I started yanking the bobby pins out. Minus this support, the hairdo stood on its own accord.

I travelled like this, in veil and jeans, to the wedding venue. At first my sister drove, but she was so wound up I asked her if she'd prefer I did. She was more nervous than me! Why? The better question is: Why wasn't I nervous?

I wasn't. I had a good solid breakfast lying in my tummy and a future with a great man ahead of me. In a couple of hours, this whole fiasco would end and I would be free. Bring it on!

Chapter Twenty two: Taking the Plunge

Marnie, the wedding planner at Pine Mansion, stormed into any room she entered. "Whatever you want," she said when Bernie arrived at Pine Mansion the morning of her wedding, "you get." She swept the wedding dress up out of Bernie's hands and swung her other arm in a windmill directing them upstairs into the bride's chamber.

Even at only four feet tall, Marnie towered over everyone. As she walked through the reception area, everyone stood to attention. Pointing and jabbing at her employees from below, Marnie seemed totally unaware of her minuscule stature, as did everyone else. With her premature grey hair and stocky figure, Marie was part army sergeant, part overbearing grandmother. More importantly, she was fighting on Bernie's team.

Marnie chomped on her gum and continued to talk as she corralled Bernie, Beth and Anne upstairs. "I know your parents, Bernadette. I remember your mother back when you turned sixteen. She called me every day for months. This time too." Marnie swept the dress up onto a hook by a long window. "But you know what? She just wants everything to be perfect." Marnie patted the dress and turned to face Bernie.

"Sit down, honey," she said. The instruction was for Bernie but they all obeyed, plopping down in unison on a plaid sofa. "I know about the whole leaving after the ceremony thing. She told me all about it. And I want you all to know that I'm going to work on her every moment to make sure she stays. But she's a stubborn woman, your mother."

"That's an understatement," Anne said.

"Hey now!" Marnie said sharply pointing at Anne with a long red nail. "I don't want any negative talk today. Think positive. This is Bernadette's day, and I'm gonna make sure everything goes smoothly."

Bernie liked Marnie. Her mother had done one thing right in arranging Pine Mansion. "Thanks," Bernie said. She stood up, feeling confident and self-assured; feeling like herself again. "I'm really looking forward to today."

Marnie punched her in the arm jovially. "That's the spirit, gal. Now you all get yourselves ready, and I'll call you when it's gettin' close to wedding time." She stormed out and down the stairs, whistling as she went.

Anne joined Bernie. "Well, you heard the woman," she said. "Let's get you dressed and married!"

*   *   *

A half-hour later and Bernadette was transformed. The dress slid over her, brushing her arms and back with silk and neatly pressing against her waist as it zipped. She glanced at her reflection and took in a small gasp of air. This was it! Her dress, her moment. Giddy, Bernie realised that in another few hours it would all be over, and the idea thrilled her.

No more talk of whether the table napkins would match the flower arrangements. No more stepping on anyone's toes. No more discussions over the seating arrangements. No more debates over chicken versus beef. No more conversations about what shape the ice sculpture should be. What does she care about ice sculptures? What does she care about any of it?

"Bring it on!" Bernie cheered to her reflection. "In a few hours I will be free, and that really is something to celebrate!"

There was a light knock on the door at the bottom of the stairs. "Yoo-hoo! Hullo?" Bernie's stepmother called up. "Is there a bride up there?"

Bernie beamed. "Yes, there is. Come on up!"

Bernie's stepmother slunk up the stairs with her hands in front of her eyes, peeking out between her fingers. "I don't want to look!" she pretended. Then squealing and throwing up her arms, "Oh! I can't help it! You're gorgeous!"

She threw her arms around Bernie and hugged her tight. "I am so proud of you, honey," she said sincerely. "This has not been easy for you." She pulled away and held out Bernie's hands. "But you're here and you're beautiful and there is a gorgeous man waiting downstairs for you. You are going to be very happy."

"Thank you," Bernie said and kissed her on the cheek. "And thanks for all your help. I hope today is as beautiful as you imagined too."

Her stepmother threw her right hand down and scoffed. "Beautiful! Ha!" She dragged Bernie over to the window. "Have you seen it down there? It is fabulous. It's like a Hollywood event. The flowers! The arrangements! The tablecloths! Incredible!"

Bernie cast her eye along the garden outside where she would marry. The chairs were set out, adorned with white, shimmering ribbons. An arch of tropical flowers cascaded like a waterfall from one side of the aisle to the other. It was truly stunning.

Beth squeezed Bernie's shoulders. "It's amazing."

Another knock interrupted them and Marnie stormed back in. "Ladies! It's almost time. You have about 15 minutes." She pointed to Bernie's stepmother. "You look almost as beautiful as our bride here! That fabric is a perfect match to the ribbons on the bridesmaids' dresses. Perfect!"

"I know!" her stepmother squealed again, ran in between Anne and Beth in their cornflower blue dresses. "I planned it that way." She gave a little spin and smiled proudly. "Now, I'm going to leave you girls to it, but just remember – enjoy!"

"I will," Bernie said with certainty. "I can't wait."

"Good, see you down there." She swept herself off and down the stairs.

Bernie turned to Marnie. "So what's left to do now?"

"There's one final decision actually," Marnie said, directing

Bernie back to the window. "Darlin', it's drizzling out there." She pointed up to the cold, grey clouds above. "Might rain. Might not. Now we can wipe those chairs down even two minutes before so that no one's bottoms get wet, but if it rains there is no cover. I still have time to bring the chairs in and do it inside. What do you want to do?"

Bernie didn't hesitate. "Let it rain," she said. "Let it rain." She laughed hard, a great belly laugh and Anne and Beth joined in. "Sorry, girls. I'm just so happy, I don't care a bit. You can all get wet, I'll be under the gazebo."

Marnie smiled. "Well, I think we might just have a bit of luck today anyway. We are thinking positive!" She turned to leave. "I'll call you in 15 minutes." Marnie swept down the stairs, bellowing to her employees as she went.

Beth licked her fingers and patted down a bit of rebellious hair from Bernie's forehead. "Do you need anything before I go?" she asked.

From head to toe, Bernie felt aglow. "No, I'll be fine. Actually, you know Beth, this may turn out to be the best day of my life after all."

Listening in, Anne smirked. "Ever the optimist." She clapped her hands together. "Right, well I'm heading down to the bathroom for one last quick pee before the ceremony. I guess I'll see you at the altar."

Bernie grasped Anne's hands before she could escape. "Thank you. Thank you so much for everything."

"Oh, you aren't going to go all sappy on me now are you?" Anne said, barely meeting Bernie's eyes because they were welling up.

"Absolutely. You're the best. You stood by me through all of this."

"Forget the last year," Anne said wiping her eyes. "I've been watching over you your whole life! It's hard work!"

Bernie laughed. "Rewarding though, right?"

"Oh, shut-up, you wedding slut, and give me a hug." They held each other, more sisters than friends. Anne gave Bernie a kiss on the cheek and held her hand.

"May I interrupt?" All the girls turned towards the stairs. Bernie's mother was standing at the bottom. Inside, Bernie felt her stomach churn with a nauseous blend of emotions.

"Mom," Beth said, her voice rising as if surprised to find her there. "I'm," she stuttered, "I'm so glad you came." She ran down the stairs to hug her.

Her mother returned the hug and then pulled away with her hands on her daughter's arms. "You look lovely, Beth."

Bernie felt what could only be described as jealousy boil inside her. Confusion and longing filled every inch of her. She nervously wiped her hands down the front of her beaded gown.

Beth looked up at Bernie and smiled. Sisters can communicate without speaking, and Bernie felt her anxiety evaporate with her sister's look of encouragement.

"May I come up, Bernadette?" their mother asked once more. Her voice was soft and deferential.

"Of course," Bernie said. Her eyes darted quickly to Anne.

Anne gave her cheek a quick peck. "Like I said, I'll see you down there." As she passed Bernie's mother on the stairwell she said, "Your daughter looks beautiful."

Her mother replied affectionately, "Yes, she does. My little girl has grown up."

Bernie's mother dabbed a tissue hidden in her palm to her eyes and Bernie noticed for the first time her mother's tears. Her eyes were puffy and her nose red. Otherwise, she was stunning. Unlike her stepmother's dress, with its perfect match to the bridesmaids' colours, her mother aimed for the opposite extreme: bright, pink fuchsia. The dress was a knock-out, trimmed in flowing bands of colour that swirled around her as she walked.

Months before, Bernie would have joked about this, in fits of giggles: "Trying to make a subtle entrance, are you?" But it was a long time since they'd laughed together. Bernie tried a different tactic. "You look great, Mom." She did too.

Her mother checked out her reflection in the mirror. "I wanted to match the flower arrangements." Bernie tried to remember how many fuchsia flowers adorned the bouquets. She had trouble recalling even one, but it was a moot point anyway.

Both women stood there, staring at the floor, saying nothing. Bernie shifted uncomfortably, playing with a loose bead on her dress.

Her mother scanned the room, finally settling on the sofa, which she sat on. Her mother could look sophisticated anywhere, even pitched demurely on the edge of an old 70s tweed sofa. "I brought you something," she said, reaching for her clutch purse and rummaging through it. She handed a small, white box to Bernie.

Bernie accepted it, a gift, in itself strange enough. Resting inside the box, on a bed of cotton padding, a pearl charm clasped a silver chain necklace.

Her mother said, "It's modern and elegant, how I like to think of you."

Bernie removed it gently from the box and turned to stand in front of the mirror. Her mother instinctively came up behind her to help fit it around her neck. She looked over Bernie's shoulder into the mirror at her daughter's reflection. "I hope," she said solemnly, "I hope you are happy, Bernadette." She patted Bernie's arm once and then let go. "I should go," she said gathering her purse from the sofa.

Bernie reached forward and kissed her on the cheek. "I love you, Mother."

Her mother wiped a tear from her eye with her tissue, but waved Bernie away. "I know. I love you too." She stroked Bernie's cheek and then glided down the stairs.

Bernie was alone. She thanked God for water-proof mascara. Moving closer to the mirror, she rubbed a tissue under her wet eyes. Then she faced her reflection one last time, clenching her fists and punching the air in front of her. "Go get 'em, tiger," she said out loud.

"Did I hear something about the Detroit Tigers?" her father called up.

"Dad! I was talking to myself, not about your baseball team."

He laughed and tore up the stairs, despite the fact that he was decked out in a tux, arms pumping at his side. When he reached the top he kept laughing. "Oh, that's right. There's another important event today besides us versus the Chicago White Sox." He took a step back. "Well, you don't look ready for batting practice, so it must be your wedding then."

Bernie giggled back at him. His laughter was contagious as usual.

"Hey wait a minute!" he cried out. "Who are you? You're gorgeous! What have you done with my daughter?" He pretended to look behind her and around the room.

Bernie obliged her father with this old joke. "It's me Dad. I'm right here!"

"Oh, wow. It is you!" He kissed her on the cheek and held her shoulders. "You look beautiful, honey." He felt in his pockets, finally locating his camera inside his jacket. "One more photo for the road," he said. She smiled, it came easy. It was her day to shine.

Once the photo was taken and the camera securely inside the tuxedo, he grew more serious. "You ready?"

"As ready as I'll ever be," she said.

"Good, because there's a whole lot of people waiting outside for you." Bernie walked to the window. The sun shone in thick beams through feeble, grey clouds. The blue sky pushed its way through, and not a single drop of rain was falling.

Her father took her arm and led her carefully down the stairs. Marnie greeted them at the bottom.

"Hello, Bride!" she said.

Bernie didn't feel nervous. She wasn't worried. She felt glorious.

"Follow me!" Marnie said, gesturing towards the door leading out to the garden. Faintly, Bernie could hear the violinist and the murmuring of the guests waiting for her. "Here's where I leave you," Marnie said in a pitched whisper. "Make your way down when you're ready. Good luck!"

Bernie gazed up at her father and he met her eyes. "Just you and me now, kid."

"Just you and I," she repeated. "I love you, Dad."

"Me too, sweetie," he said, kissing her on the cheek. "Now remember, there's no crying in baseball."

Bernie laughed and together they began the procession. As soon as they were sighted, everyone stood to attention, looking solemn as fit the ceremony.

As he reached the arch, her father called out to the guests. "Don't worry," he said. "The Tigers are winning 3-2." Everyone burst out laughing. Her father whispered to her. "I want everyone to be wearing a smile like yours today."

Bernie caught Sam's eye. He walked forward to meet her. He grasped her father's hand and shook it solidly. Then he took her arm in his. "You look beautiful," he whispered.

Each step brought her closer and closer to the end of the wedding and the beginning of her life with Sam. She looked across the field of guests and found Sam's parents. His mother used a delicate handkerchief to wipe away a tear and his dad gave her an encouraging smile and wave. Then Bernie caught her sister's eye. Lashed with tears and makeup ruined, Beth sobbed uncontrollably. Momentarily, Bernie left Sam and hugged her sister.

"I just can't believe it," Beth stuttered through gasping breaths. "I'm going to miss you so much."

"I'm going to miss you too. Here," she passed Beth a cloth handkerchief, the 'something new' Anne gave her just before the wedding for such a moment. "I love you, Little B."

Beth kissed her, still sobbing, "Love you too, Big B." Beth blew furiously into the handkerchief and resumed her place in the wedding procession.

Finally, Bernie's mother stepped forward. She took Bernie in her arms and gave her the first real hug they'd shared since their separation. "I love you, Bernadette," her mother said.

They pulled apart and Bernadette turned to Sam, her own eyes tearing up. She took his hand in her own. "I'm ready," she said firmly. The rabbi made a gesture and everyone sat down.

Bernie took Sam's hand in hers. She watched with amazement as Sam concentrated on the rabbi's voice, glancing at her off and on to give her a comforting smile. The significance of the ceremony hit her, but even in her joy, she felt stiff. Suddenly, she realised her butt cheeks were clenched so tight, she could crush diamonds between them.

Relax, buttocks, she thought to herself. *Relax, buttocks, relax.*

Her butt unclenched, and so did she. Bernie loved it. She loved Sam. She looked around and realised that despite everything, she had made the right decision. Not the wedding! No, way. She should have eloped.

No, it was Sam. He was the best decision she had ever made. She gripped his hand and, gleaming, she met his eyes. She knew he felt the same. When they exchanged their vows, they meant every one. When they were given permission to kiss, he kissed her long and deep and pressed her to him.

The rabbi encouraged cheers of "Mazel Tov!", Hebrew for congratulations, as Sam led his new wife back down the aisle. Everyone applauded, and Bernie felt all her cares and worries leave her at the altar as she made her way into the reception.

*   *   *

Moments later, Sam and Bernie were surrounded by well wishers. As she kissed and thanked everyone for coming, she felt none of the embarrassment she was expecting after all the trauma of the last few months.

Then her mother placed her hand lightly on her arm. She asked, "Bernadette, could I speak with you?"

Bernie followed her mother into a small alcove, shutting the door behind them. "It's time for us to go," her mother said. Bernie looked at her mother's eyes, pleading with her daughter to ask her to stay.

So Bernie did. "Stay, enjoy the party. You know my stepmother set aside a table for you and your guests just in case."

Her mother shook her head, "No, no we can't. It's not for us. It's not our dream for you. It's your stepmother's vision, not yours or ours." She looked downcast and Bernie didn't know what to say. After experiencing the ceremony, Bernie wondered how anyone could feel she wasn't a part of this day.

Marnie poked her head through the door. "Everyone is taking their seats. We'll be calling you in a minute. You better go back out to Sam now."

This moment seemed to represent the whole wedding for Bernie. She was saying good-bye to her childhood, to the protective envelope of her mother and stepping into the rest of her life, one she hoped was filled with as much joy and excitement as she felt now. "I have to go now, Mother," she said. "But, I want you to know, I love you. I hope you believe me."

Her mother wept, and held Bernie to her. "Be happy Bernadette," she said. They rested there for a moment and then her mother turned and went.

Bernie opened the door and greeted her future.

Wedding Truth No. 23

A wedding is painful enough. Wear comfortable shoes.

If you take any of my advice, take this. If you ignore everything I say – which let's be honest you probably will – if you insist on your way, if you don't elope, if you (gasp!) try to buy your own invitations, please I beg you: listen to this advice. Comfortable shoes can be the difference between a reception you dance through or limp through.

I had the most beautiful shoes for my wedding. My mom bought them for me. They were white sandals adorned in the same material as my dress. The straps lightly graced my ankles and the heel wasn't even that high. No one saw them. They were under my dress.

Little did I know how these shoes would conspire to attack me following the ceremony. How could I know they were designed to disable me? The silky padding of those sandals forced my feet to nose-dive off the sharp edges of the soles and those light straps strangled my ankles in a death grip, cutting into my legs until swollen, red welts appeared. Not attractive. Not comfortable.

As soon as the photographer released me, I ran back upstairs to my changing room and into my trainers. As a wedding accessory, my trainers were hardly appropriate. I'd owned them for three years. They were grey (their actual colour, not acquired with age) and filthy with muddy remnants I'd collected during morning runs.

Still, I wore them and said a silent prayer of thanks to the designers at Adidas. Did anyone notice? My ring-bearer did, but he was the only one and he was thrilled.

Test those shoes out, ladies. Weddings are a painful business and the party afterwards shouldn't be.

Epilogue: ...and they all lived happily ever after.

An accident waiting to happen. Eminent disaster. Relationship suicide. These are the kind of phrases my sister and I chose to use when discussing my wedding.

We still discuss it. Years later, emotions still burn near the surface in regards to the circus that my wedding became. We laugh about it too; that's what sisters do for one another.

I was lucky enough to have someone like my sister, who knew intimately the difficult terrain of my family. Though younger, my sister has always seen me through the most difficult of familial situations. It was she on the phone to both my parents, long after I had given up, trying to mend their differences with each other and with me. It was she who listened to me cry well into the night. It was she that screamed at me the words I didn't want to hear, that my wedding wasn't as important as keeping my family together. She was right. She usually is.

After the wedding, in long late-night overseas conversations, we contemplated the future of my relationship with my mother. My sister always encouraged me to remain in contact with her, and I thank her for that. Admittedly for years, it was challenging. Both my mother and I felt wronged, both waited for apologies that never came, both felt out of place in a relationship so crucial to our lives. But we did it. Essentially, we are very different people who learned to cope the best we can. It helps that we care about each other. As my Dad is fond of saying, you can pick your nose, but you can't pick your family.

Regardless, I'm pleased with the way things have turned out now. My mother has visited me in London, and she adores my husband, as does my whole family. I love her and I never want her out of my life again. I don't agree with the decisions she made, but I understand why she made them. It is frightening to say goodbye to your daughter. I should have told her how frightening it was for me to say goodbye as well. Needless to say, even though I wish I had never put myself through it, I love being married. Certainly the moral of this tale isn't: Don't get married.

After all I went through, my sister certainly didn't learn that. She got married herself two years ago. He's a great guy and, while I'm sure my parents appreciated that he has not one blue hair or earring in sight, he is so obviously in love with her, liking him was easy.

Planning her wedding wasn't all roses for her either. She negotiated some rocky roads as well. But see, she's smart, my sister:

1. She learned from my mistakes and got married out of state, away from our parents' favourite florists.

2. Since she was in a different state, she didn't have to entertain guests she didn't know. Only people close to her or our family were invited.

3. She paid for much more than I was able to, giving herself a major say over what happened.

4. She chose a place where they hand you a preference list to tick off your choices. From photographer to cake design, the decisions are taken out of your (and your parents) hands.

Where is this magical place where parents have less control over what happens at their daughter's wedding? Walt Disney World.

Two years ago my sister walked down the aisle of the Disney wedding chapel in Florida. Cinderella's Castle glowed white in the distance behind her and not a single family member arrived upset.

I used the same handkerchief in her wedding to dab my eyes as I carried in my own. There is nothing better than watching the union of two people you love, knowing they will support each other and be friends with each other for the rest of their lives.

I know what you are thinking. She made a trade off for this

peaceful union: a tacky, cartoon wedding. My sister is too intelligent and sentimental for that. Her wedding was as romantic, beautiful and elegant as mine. Even more so, since our mother actually stayed for the whole event.

I'd like to congratulate my sister. A toast: May we all find as much happiness, love and joy in our lives as she found in hers that day.

And one last maxim for the road:

Wedding Truth No. 23

A wedding is just a big party. The next day you wake up hungover.

A marriage is the rest of your life. If you choose right, every day you'll wake up in love.

Acknowledgements

I wish to thank my parents and stepparents who accepted the publication of this book with humour and love. For the record, I would like to point out that this experience with them is only a small portion of my life. They have offered me more support and love than I can possibly describe here.

I would also like to thank Carrie Parson, Dani Littlejohn and Michele Roger for reading over the book in its various stages and offering many ideas I subsequently pilfered. Carrie, your 'insider perspective' was especially appreciated. Also to Julia Svoboda, my unofficial editor since I met her at 13, who assisted me on this and every other project I've ever attempted. And to everyone at Snowbooks who took a chance on my story.

Many thanks as well to all those people who helped me get through my wedding, especially Maggie, Idris, Peter and Jennifer Griffiths who have always made me feel like family, as well as Anthony, Tina, Gavin, Michelle, Carl, Ruth, and Kate.

Finally, no one deserves more thanks than my husband, who went through the whole experience with me and managed not to kill anyone. Thank God we'll never have to go through this again, Gareth. Thank God.

Author Info

Stacie Lewis grew up in the suburbs of Detroit. She wrote a popular wedding diary for a British web site and has also written for several magazines and newspapers including regular contributions to the Detroit News. She lives in London with her husband.

Visit her website at: http://www.stacielewis.com/